D0430799

" 'And they call that thing a petticoat!' "—*Page 233*

ROAST BEEF, MEDIUM

THE BUSINESS ADVENTURES
OF EMMA McCHESNEY

EDNA FERBER

Introduction by Lawrence R. Rodgers
Illustrated by James Montgomery Flagg

University of Illinois Press
Urbana and Chicago

Library of Congress Cataloging-in-Publication Data
Ferber, Edna, 1887–1968.
Roast beef, medium : the business adventures of Emma
McChesney / Edna Ferber ; introduction by
Lawrence R. Rodgers ; illustrated by
James Montgomery Flagg.
p.   cm.
Includes bibliographical references.
ISBN 0-252-02645-4 (alk. paper)
ISBN 0-252-06945-5 (pbk. : alk. paper)
1. McChesney, Emma (Fictitious character)—Fiction.
2. Businesswomen—Fiction.
3. Adventure stories, American.
4. United States—Social life and customs—
20th century—Fiction.
I. Title
PS3511.E46R63   2001
813'.52—DC21   00-061510

1 2 3 4 5 C P 5 4 3 2 1

CONTENTS

PAGE

INTRODUCTION BY
LAWRENCE R. RODGERS ix

FOREWORD xxix

I. ROAST BEEF, MEDIUM 1

II. REPRESENTING T. A. BUCK 28

III. CHICKENS 50

IV. HIS MOTHER'S SON 78

V. PINK TIGHTS AND GINGHAMS . . . 107

VI. SIMPLY SKIRTS 137

VII. UNDERNEATH THE HIGH-CUT VEST . . 166

VIII. CATCHING UP WITH CHRISTMAS . . . 196

IX. KNEE-DEEP IN KNICKERS 230

X. IN THE ABSENCE OF THE AGENT . . . 263

ILLUSTRATIONS

" 'And they call that thing a petticoat!' " . *Frontispiece*

PAGE

" 'Peter Piper picked a peck of pickled peppers,' he announced, glibly" 5

" 'That was a married kiss—a two-year-old married kiss at least' " 15

" 'I won't ask you to forgive a hound like me' " . . 25

" 'You'll never grow up, Emma McChesney' " . . . 57

" 'Well, s'long then, Shrimp. See you at eight' " . . 63

" 'I'm still in a position to enforce that ordinance against pouting ' " 69

" 'Son!' echoed the clerk, staring" 81

" 'Well!' gulped Jock, 'those two double-bedded, bloomin', blasted Bisons—' " 91

" 'Come on out of here and I'll lick the shine off your shoes, you blue-eyed babe, you!' " 103

" 'You can't treat me with your life's history. I'm going in' " 115

" 'Now, Lillian Russell and cold cream is one; and new potatoes and brown crocks is another' " . . . 127

" 'Why, girls, I couldn't hold down a job in a candy factory' " 133

" 'Honestly, I'd wear it myself!' " 151

" 'I've lived petticoats, I've talked petticoats, I've dreamed petticoats—why, I've even worn the darn things!' " 157

"And found himself addressing the backs of the letters on the door marked 'Private' " 163

ILLUSTRATIONS

PAGE

" 'Shut up, you blamed fool! Can't you see the lady's sick?' " 169

"At his gaze that lady fled, sample-case banging at her knees" 185

"In the exuberance of his young strength, he picked her up" 191

"She read it again, dully, as though every selfish word had not already stamped itself on her brain and heart" 205

" 'Not that you look your age—not by ten years!' " . . . . *Facing page* 218

" 'Christmas isn't a season . . . it's a feeling; and, thank God, I've got it!' " 227

" 'No man will ever appreciate the fine points of this little garment, but the women—' " *Facing page* 250

" 'Emma McChesney . . . I believe in you now! Dad and I both believe in you' " 259

"It had been a whirlwind day" 265

" 'Emma,' he said, 'will you marry me?' " 285

" 'Welcome home!' she cried. 'Sketch in the furniture to suit yourself' " . . . . . *Facing page* 288

INTRODUCTION
Lawrence R. Rodgers

In early 1911, twenty-six-year-old Edna Ferber wrote a story about a commercial traveler, a "woman drummer," named Emma McChesney. She sent it to Bert Boyden, the editor of one of the day's more popular women's journals, *American Magazine*. With no real expectations for success, she immediately began a new story about a scrubwoman in a Chicago office building. By all standards Ferber was still a fledgling writer, having sold her first work, "The Homely Heroine," just two years earlier to *Everybody's Magazine* for $50.60. But her scrubwoman tale never saw completion. To Ferber's surprise, Emma was an instant hit, prompting Boyden to ask Ferber for a series of stories. Despite her doubts about having anything more to say about a character whose world was far afield from her own, Ferber came up with another story that, in her words, "named itself Roast Beef Medium" and became "a turning point in my writing life."[1] (The title refers to the comfort food experienced commercial travelers eat, setting them apart from the newcomers who choose exotic and unhealthy fare.) Before Emma McChesney's five-year magazine run was complete, she would become one of the country's favorite fictional personalities, and the author would experience the first taste of fame and wealth that would follow her through the rest of her prolific career.[2]

The stories generated enough interest to lead to three collected volumes, *Roast Beef, Medium* (1913), *Personality Plus* (1914), and *Emma McChesney & Co.* (1915). They had the added benefit of pen-and-ink drawings by James Montgomery Flagg, a leading periodical illustrator, whose popular images of young women were known as "Flagg Girls." A poster designer during World War I, he is best remembered for his "Uncle Sam Wants You" World War II recruitment poster. His illustrations of Emma dovetail nicely with Ferber's text. The artist's focus is on Emma's fashionable garb and her facial expression, which allow Flagg to showcase his subject's charm and command of her setting. An equally sympathetic version of Emma's tale made its way to Broadway's Lyceum Theatre in 1915 as *Our Mrs. McChesney* for a run of 152 performances with Emma played by the leading lady of the day, Ethel Barrymore. The stage adaptation had been written by Ferber and George V. Hobart, a noted librettist, vaudeville sketch writer, and one of the era's more productive dramatists. And while Ferber found the glamorous and elegant Barrymore miscast, complaining privately that the actress upstaged her own animated creation, Ferber knew enough, in the midst of a Broadway hit, to keep such opinions to herself.

Readers new to Ferber and to *Roast Beef, Medium*, which has been out of print for nearly three decades, will find it a remarkably contemporary collection. Its preoccupation with Emma McChesney's struggle to balance the competing demands of work and home brings to the surface many of the same issues that fuel contemporary debates. When we first meet Emma, she is a divorced mother in her midthirties who has been living out of a suitcase for the past ten years as a representative of T. A. Buck's Featherloom Petticoat Company. She has a seventeen-year-old son, Jock, who is as charming, handsome, and frustratingly irresponsible as his "worthless father" (181). She is America's first businesswoman in literature. And she is typical of the many strong women who would populate Ferber's later writings: independent, outspoken, witty, a feminist. "Emma was," in the words of Ferber's biographer, "just as much a major statement about and a breakthrough for women, as she was an engaging serial to follow (skirting the corners of what we now define as 'soap opera')."[3] Although Emma is immensely likable, her success is tied less to her personality (the stock capital of the sales business) than to her solid work ethic. The connection between toil and achievement would emerge as one of Ferber's prevalent themes.[4] The most accomplished seller in a company—and a profession—dominated by men, Emma, "who had forgotten more about petticoats than the average skirt salesman ever knew," gets up earlier, travels further, and puts in more hours than her competitors (3).

Frequently, the stories' social commentary, and their humor, derive from Ferber's subversion of gender expectations. "'Emma McChesney,' announces her gruff but lovable boss, T. A. Buck, 'you ought to have been a man. With that head on a man's shoulders, you could put us out of business.' 'I could do it anyway,' Mrs. McChesney had retorted" (199). Time and again Emma must deal with men who underestimate her mental faculties, her talent for selling, and, especially, her low tolerance for their assumption that she is forlorn, defenseless, and in need of their protection. Or the men are attracted to her beauty and make inappropriate advances. Or they make a proclamation about the limitations and propensities of women in general, the falsity of which Emma promptly demonstrates. "A woman don't like to buy of a woman," announces Ed Meyers, Emma's chief competitor and antagonist, shortly before he loses another woman's account to her (145). Ferber's feminist notions are not without complication. She wants women to be measured by their competencies, yet can appear more concerned with their physical appeal (or lack thereof) than their abilities. In her world, beautiful women triumph over plain ones. One of Emma's female antagonists is a "flat-chested, thin-haired" woman who hates Emma for wearing "a large thirty-six without one inch of alteration" (138). Her congenial doctor is characteristically "handsome" (171), while the less likable Ed Meyers is "fat" (176). If such intimations of character appear superficial to present readers, they did not seem to trouble Ferber, who appears intent on allowing Emma to employ whatever resources are to her benefit. And there is a payoff, for in an era when women had little agency in the workplace, Emma sets her own terms.

One might imagine Emma McChesney occupying a nearly impossible position, perched precariously between the male world of selling, with all of its complex codes of masculine behavior, its vices, and its stereotypes, and the female domestic world, which is so distant from the small-town hotels that she often calls home. A potential buyer in one of her later stories characterizes her position as an either/or choice: "A woman cannot be really charming and also capable in business."[5] The basis of her appeal, however, as well as her thoroughly modern sensibility, is that she is anything but liminal. Gliding effortlessly between marketing and motherhood, between dry goods stores and sewing parlors, "Emma McChesney would make a Pullman car snowbound at Winnipeg look as domestic as the Old Homestead."[6] She was, as Ferber created her, the new century's ideal woman, a model melding of character traits, skills, and opportunities that gratified the liberatory fantasies of even her most homebound women readers. Ferber herself summarized the response of her target audience: "She knows that Emma McChesney could mix a devil's food cake and ice it just as successfully as she could approach a grouchy customer in Dubuque, Iowa, or carry on a conversation that has to do with books and music and philosophy."[7] It is worth noting that Emma had her male fans as well. Her loyal following included Theodore Roosevelt, who reportedly asked Ferber the first time he met her in 1912, "What are you going to do about Emma McChesney?" His intent apparently was to urge Emma toward a more conventional social role. As he would later tell Ferber in a letter: "Of course I have read all those stories. . . . I wonder if you feel that I am hopelessly sentimental because my only objection to the last twelve pages is that I would have liked somehow to see not only the boy marry, but poor Emma McChesney at last have the chance herself to marry somebody decent with whom she was in love."[8]

According to Ferber, however, women liked Emma single,

and those most in the know found her authentic. Traveling saleswomen penned letters to tell her so. "I am the woman you are writing about," wrote one. "How did you come to know so much about me?"[9] Ferber had a gift for delineating others' lives, yet it is hardly surprising that saleswomen wanted to embrace so idealized a portrait of their own small world. Although women dominated the ranks of those working behind store counters, a woman who took to the road to peddle her wares was as rare in real life as she was in fiction. Throughout the nineteenth century, women constituted only 1 to 2 percent of the ranks of traveling salespeople.[10] Ferber's closest personal encounter came through a story her mother told of a mouse-trap-selling woman who visited the family store in Appleton, Wisconsin. Apart from Emma's ability to beat her male counterparts at their own game, she bears little professional resemblance to salesmen—real or fictional—and thus avoids bearing the disagreeable baggage of their trade.

As a group, traveling men had a raffish and uncouth reputation. Rendered through an array of colorful stereotypes, they were favorite targets of satire and caricatured in films, plays, novels, and even dirty jokes as drunks, gamblers, and womanizers. Their homes were seedy small-town hotels. They eschewed families for the loose fraternity of other men of the road. The ubiquity of their presence in small-town America between 1830 and 1920 is largely lost on contemporary readers. The decade in which Ferber created Emma represented a critical juncture, even an endpoint, in the traveling man's evolution, as he began to move from the stereotyped "old-time drummer" to the modern salesman, who downplayed his individuality in favor of standardized selling practices. The former's command of the marketplace depended on the kind of face-to-face interaction that is Emma's stock-in-trade. The shift to the latter's new commercial methods is reflected in the frontispiece of a 1912 book on advertising that dedicates itself to "American businessmen who successfully apply science where their predecessors were confined to custom."[11] If the traveling salesman was a highly visible, if coarse, wing of commerce that helped set twentieth-century consumer culture into motion, the salesman's gradual demise since then is an indication of the advancing facelessness of this same consumer culture—the transition from person-to-person conversation to the dialogue of the small-town storefront, the suburban shopping mall, the mass-mailed catalog, and, finally, the Internet portal.

The salesman's status as a member of one of the country's most visible groups of ordinary working folk has been transformed into a larger-than-life presence on the page. The male commercial traveler has always been a conspicuous, symbolically freighted figure among American writers. He has embodied both the American obsession with self-creation and the twentieth century's preoccupation with democracy as an enterprise manifested through commercial communities. In one sense, the salesman's identity can be expressed as a tautology: who he is depends on his product and his public, yet the product he touts is always himself, an audience of one. He is, like Arthur Miller's totemic Willy Loman, "way out there in the blue, riding on a smile and a shoeshine."[12] From Theodore Dreiser's oily Drouet in *Sister Carrie,* Eudora Welty's lamentable R. J. Bowman in "Death of a Traveling Salesman," and Flannery O'Connor's deceitful Manley Pointer in "Good Country People" through the men in David Mamet's *Glengarry Glen Ross,* salesmen have been depicted as mythic, always flawed figures. Ferber is linked to this group by her interest both in representing Emma as a vestige of the old-fashioned, personality-based seller and in documenting the individual tolls exacted by this profession.

But the similarities end at the personal level. Where all of these writers examine commercial culture critically, Ferber adopts an upbeat, pro-business ethos. Ferber was not unaware of these larger cultural issues facing traveling men. However, the slow decline of their importance held little interest for her when compared with the burgeoning opportunities that American business held for women in general. Emma's popularity turned Ferber into a national advocate for all business-women and provided her with prominent forums to air her views. Her most extensive set of opinions on the subject appeared in a piece by Joyce Kilmer, "Business Woman Most Domestic," in the April 4, 1915, issue of the *New York Times Magazine.* Ferber's basic point is enough in line with her stories that one can imagine Emma making the following speech:

> They're as modern as the Woolworth Building, these business women of today. But they're as wholesome, and sane, and womanly as their mothers or grandmothers before them. You'll find them at the heads of departments, you'll find them as foreign buyers, you'll find them selling goods on the road, in insurance offices, in real estate offices. Quiet, capable, well-dressed, poised. I love them. I like their humor. I admire their courage. They

know so much about life, which means they are so tolerant of men and women. Knowledge doesn't sour them. It mellows them. They're sympathetic and human and lovable. Show me a successful business woman between 30 and 40 years of age, and I'll show you as charming, and witty, and broad-minded and companionable a woman as there is in the world.[13]

Ferber's optimism suggests not only her pro-woman advocacy but also that she was a product of her age. She embraced the liberal wing of progressivism's potential. Throughout her life, though capable of measured critique, she time and again expressed belief in the efficacy of large American institutions, whether political, social, or commercial, as crucial instruments in making life better, fairer, and more democratic for all. When Ferber created Emma, the tenuous equilibrium of capitalistic competition and democratic processes seemed momentarily in balance: women were on their way to voting, the excesses of the Gilded Age had been somewhat curbed, and Germany appeared very far away. Although he would not make the statement for another decade, Calvin Coolidge's pronouncement that "the business of America is business" was a dictum Ferber had already espoused.

❖

Looking back, Ferber once claimed to have no explanation for why she happened on a character like Emma McChesney. Ferber's upbringing, however, provides ample clues. She was born, the second of two daughters, on August 15, 1885, in Kalamazoo, Michigan. Her father, Jacob Charles, was a first-generation Hungarian-Jewish immigrant, her mother, Julia

Newman, a second-generation German Jew with Chicago roots. "Completely engulfed by his family of three energetic high-vitality females," Ferber's father was a genial shopowner, "a decent, dull rather handsome man," in Ferber's words, with little interest in or aptitude for business. It fell on "that indomitable woman, Julia Ferber, my mother," to oversee her parents' general store, which they operated in Ottumwa, Iowa, from 1890 to 1897.[14] In Ottumwa she experienced daily episodes of anti-Semitism, which had the effect of turning her inward and bookish and making her appreciative of the tough-minded sensibility—so often present in the characters of her books—that could stave off such attacks. Emma McChesney displays no overt traces of her author's Jewish background. Why Ferber seems to suppress her character's ethnic identity is worth further speculation. It may well be that Ferber—whose Americanness, more than her Jewishness, dominated her sense of self—simply didn't want to subsume her character within an identity that risked limiting her broad appeal. Which is not to say that Ferber shied away from her Jewish heritage or controversial material. In *Fanny Herself*, her 1917 semiautobiographical novel, she would focus on the especially strong adaptive qualities of a Jewish girl growing up in a small midwestern town. Her 1939 autobiography, *A Peculiar Treasure*, was written as a direct response to the world's growing fear of Nazism and fascism.

From Ottumwa, Ferber's family moved to the more progressive town of Appleton, Wisconsin, where she graduated from high school and became the first female writer for the *Appleton Daily Crescent*. She took the job out of necessity when her father developed eye problems that eventually rendered him blind. Her stint as a reporter was not easy. In Appleton, she endured the criticism of townspeople who found journalism a distasteful trade for a woman. After relocating to Milwaukee for a better reporting job, she suffered what was called a "nervous collapse" and had to return home, not long after the death of her father, to the capable, caring hands of her mother.

Ferber's feelings about the contrast between her weak father and strong mother worked themselves out over a lifetime of writing. As her biographer, Julie Goldsmith Gilbert (who, as Ferber's grandniece, possesses personal insight into family matters), claimed: "Every Ferber heroine had young Julia's qualities. Almost every Ferber fictional male owned Jacob's deficiencies."[15] Ferber's recollections of her mother, which were clouded by a perennial ambivalence about her dominating personality, are spelled out in a tribute to Julia she composed shortly after her death. The resemblance to Emma McChesney is striking: "She had self reliance, courage, fortitude, humor, intelligence, and a sense of values that was almost too keen."[16] Ferber imagined other less immediate sources for Emma, among them Ida Tarbell, the prominent muck-raking journalist for *McClure's*, or a more general category of women, the once-prissy southern lady who, after the Civil War, "rolled up her sleeves, put on a gingham apron and really got to work."[17] But, ultimately, it is a glorified version of "Julia McFerber," as Edna's mother more than once called herself, that best serves as Emma's alter ego.

Ferber's success with Emma McChesney seemed, in one

sense, to breed only more success. Specializing in carefully researched panoramic novels that encapsulated moments and places in American history, Ferber emerged as one of the dominant regionalists of the twentieth century. However, despite a five-decade run of impressive commercial achievement, Ferber never attained significant recognition from the literary establishment, who relegated her writing to that category of books that were, in their time, prominent and interesting, but not of sufficient depth to sustain the label "classic." By this standard, which carries its own biases, what is lacking in her work are characters who have the dense psychological depth found in the fiction of other prominent writers of the period, such as Edith Wharton, Willa Cather, and Sherwood Anderson. However much Ferber was, like these writers, able to embody the particular spirit of a place and time, she was not especially interested in attending to the inner terrain of the characters who inhabit her small universes. While her *New York Times* obituary acknowledged her as "among the best-read novelists in the nation," it also declared that "her books were not profound but they were vivid and had a sound sociological basis."[18] Over the years, Ferber had stared down her share of similar critiques with little apparent damage to her artistic ego—mostly because, as she liked to point out, she wrote for her devoted readers, not for critics.

And wrote she did. *Roast Beef, Medium* was her third book. After debuting in 1911 with *Dawn O'Hara*, which Julia Ferber had rescued from the trash, and *Buttered Side Down*, a 1912 collection whose style reviewers likened to that of O. Henry, Ferber went on to write thirteen novels, nine plays, two autobiographies, and nine other collections of stories, as well as overseeing twenty-five of her works sold for film treatments. *So Big,* her story of turn-of-the-century Chicago, won the 1924 Pulitzer Prize. Her 1926 *Show Boat* provided the basis for what many still consider Broadway's most influential musical. *Cimarron* was the best-selling American novel for 1930. Thereafter followed *American Beauty* (1931), which touched on two hundred years of Connecticut history; *Come and Get It* (1935), a similarly sweeping look at Michigan and Wisconsin; *Giant* (1952), her most notorious, and popular, regional novel, whose wide-open Texas landscape became the backdrop to a film starring James Dean, Rock Hudson, and Elizabeth Taylor; and *Ice Palace* (1958), Ferber's last novel, which contributed to the kind of substantial public awareness that Alaska needed to ease its transition from a remote and strange territory into a bona fide addition to the American republic.

The vast scope of Ferber's material was both the basis and the bane of her critical reputation. On the one hand, as regionalist, multiculturalist, and feminist, she covered untapped ground in her effort to showcase the diverse range of American character. She advocated on behalf of Native Americans, extolled the virtue of the working class, and condemned the treatment of Mexicans in Texas. On the other hand, her method for writing her books cast her in the perpetual role of outsider. She took great pride in her ability to enter a world not her own (that of the commercial traveler was the first instance)—to observe it, research it, and emerge with a best-seller that, to her mind, penetrated the very heart of its regional psyche. While she was terribly sure of her singular gift, adopting it as her own "peculiar treasure" (the title of her 1939 autobiography, also a best-seller), the insiders were not always so captivated.

The reception of *Cimarron* is a case in point. During a spring 1927 visit to the Kansas home of her good friend William Allen White, Ferber listened with rapt fascination to a conversation centering on a driving trip White, his wife, and their son took the previous autumn through Oklahoma. Ferber recalled that White's "trained reportorial nose had missed nothing of the fantastic, the dramatic, the tragic, the absurd in the bizarre commonwealth so newly oil-rich." "What a novel!" Ferber exclaimed. "Why hasn't someone written about it?" Begging off the subject herself, she claimed it was too big a canvas filled with too much open space. "Too hard work," she announced. What she was after were stories about "two people in a telephone booth." Nonetheless, she jumped at White's offer to have, in her words, a "tourist's look" at the young state. And as soon as "mud-wallows out in the oil-country" dried out later that spring, she returned to Kansas and drove south, where, during her thirteen-day visit, Ferber realized that the hot, exasperating, fascinating landscape she beheld must become the panorama of her next novel.[19]

With the trip behind her, she turned the story of frontier Oklahoma into what reviewers labeled an "American Rhapsody" and a "gorgeous piece of work."[20] Her two principals were a restless small-town newspaper man, Yancey Cravate, whose physical splendor and brash spirit anticipated many a later western movie hero, and Yancey's wife, Sabra, a headstrong pioneer heroine who bore a notable resemblance to one of the state's favored daughters, Elva Shartel Ferguson, wife of Territorial Governor Thomson B. Ferguson. Through Yancey and Sabra, readers hit all the benchmarks of prestatehood history. There is the famous April 1889 one-day land grab; the clashing of sooners and boomers; the discovery of oil; the undercurrent of Native American exploitation; the colorful bandits, speculators, surveyors, politicians, ministers, and claim lawyers—all set amid the rapidly diminishing frontier. The novel remains the most enduring literary vessel of romanticized images touching on this crucial era in the region's history. Following a hugely successful serial in *Women's Home Companion*, *Cimarron* became 1930's number one best-seller. As one Cleveland bookseller gushed to Ferber: "If we cannot make a record on [*Cimarron*], I give up."[21] The half million copies sold over the next five years were helped along by a 1931 movie featuring Richard Dix and Irene Dunne that won the Academy Award for best picture.

But to Ferber's surprise, many Oklahomans greeted the book with hostility. Noting a general air of superiority during her visit which seemed to have "entitled her to special privileges in rudeness," they denounced the novel, wrote angry editorials, pecked at even the tiniest of her historical inaccuracies, and generally grumbled about an outsider's audacity in trying to represent a time and place not her own.[22] The meanest volley came from a Bartlesville paper, which remembered her as "an extremely offensive personality garnished with a profusion of hair dye and egotism."[23] Ferber's cantankerous nature would have fueled such reactions, but it was her temerity in claiming to speak for them and know their lives that underpinned the people of Oklahoma's real frustration.

No such reactions greeted Emma McChesney, in part because her stories did not pretend to meet the standard of verisimilitude that would be applied to her historical fiction. Emma was also an optimistic and generally positive character who embodied the kind of woman that men desired and other women wanted to be. In fact, when Ferber finally decided to retire the McChesney series, she did so despite her sizable audience's eagerness for more stories. Her third book, *Emma McChesney & Co.,* had been generally greeted as enthusiastically as its predecessors. "According to all the rules of precedent," wrote a *New York Times* reviewer, "one should by now be thoroughly tired of Emma McChesney," yet Ferber still delivered "one of the most humorous and original love stories that has appeared for years."[24] In this volume Emma would become a grandmother, she would try unsuccessfully to quit work and become a lady of leisure, and she would marry T. A. Buck Jr. Although such developments showcased the interesting changes and growth that Ferber captured over the many stories she wrote about Emma, they also turned her into a more conventional, less daring heroine.

In the meantime, Ferber was becoming worried that Emma would take over her own identity. Thus when the editor of *Cosmopolitan* wrote to ask for more stories—twenty, or as many as she would write—she did not automatically say yes. Emma was so popular that Ferber's contract let her set her own price and terms, and she knew she could continue writing the stories "with eyes shut and one hand tied behind [her]." But, as she reports in *A Peculiar Treasure,* one memorable line from a review made her decision for her: "Edna Ferber . . . in her latest volume of the saga of the traveling saleswoman is evidently keeping Emma McChesney alive with injections of black ink." After staring at the sentence for a long time, she recognized that even if her readers loved Emma, she found truth in the review. It was time to move on, so she sent the contract back: "I know now that if I had signed that contract I never should have advanced as a writer and probably never would have written a fresh line again in all my life."[25] The productive career that lay ahead makes such words sound less like a real prognosis than the exaggerated appraisal of a writer suffering momentary character fatigue.

Fortunately, present readers will have no such reactions. In *Roast Beef, Medium,* they meet Emma in her freshest and earliest form, while Ferber was still enamored of her character. And like her early audiences, Ferber's new readers will find much pleasure in this first representative of a long progression of spirited Ferber heroines.

Notes

1. Edna Ferber, *A Peculiar Treasure* (New York: Doubleday, Doran, 1939), 173.

2. Sources for information about Ferber's career include her two autobiographies, *A Peculiar Treasure* and *A Kind of Magic* (New York: Doubleday, 1963). See also Julie Goldsmith Gilbert, *Ferber: A Biography* (Garden City, N.Y.: Doubleday, 1978); Steven P. Horowitz and Miriam J. Landsman, "Edna Ferber," in *Dictionary of Literary Biography: Twentieth-Century American Jewish Fiction Writers,* ed. Daniel Walden (Detroit: Gale Research, 1984), 28:58–64; and Ellen Serlen Uffen, "Edna Ferber," in *Dictionary of Literary Biography: American Short-Story Writers, 1910–1945,* ed. Bobby Ellen Kimbel (Detroit: Gale Research, 1992), 86:91–98.

3. Gilbert, *Ferber,* 408.

4. Ferber addresses her own obsession with work in *A Peculiar Treasure:* "With millions of others I have been a work worshiper. Work and more work. Work was a sedative, a stimulant, an escape, an exercise, a diversion, a passion. When friends failed or fun palled or spirits flagged, there was my typewriter and there was the world, my oyster. I've worked daily for over a quarter of a century, and loved it. I've worked while ill in bed, while travel-ing in Europe, riding on trains. I've written in woodsheds, bathrooms, cab-ins, compartments, bedrooms, living rooms, gardens, porches, decks, ho-tels, newspaper offices, theaters, kitchens. Nothing in my world was so satisfactory, so lasting and sustaining as work" (11).

5. Edna Ferber, "Broadway to Buenos Aires," *Emma McChesney & Co.* (New York: Frederick A. Stokes, 1915).

6. Joyce Kilmer, "Business Woman Most Domestic," *New York Times Magazine,* Apr. 4, 1915, 4.

7. Edna Ferber, "Hats Off to the Business Woman!" *New York Times,* Oct. 24, 1915, sec. 6, p. 6.

8. Qtd. in Gilbert, *Ferber,* 408–9.

9. Kilmer, "Business Woman Most Domestic," 5. See also Ferber, "Hats Off to the Business Woman!" 6.

10. Timothy B. Spears, *One Hundred Years on the Road: The Traveling Salesman in American Culture* (New Haven: Yale University Press, 1995), 145. Spears's book is an invaluable source on the general importance of the trav-eling salesman's role in shaping American culture. See especially 7–12. For a useful critical examination of Emma McChesney as a female worker, see William Gleason, "'Find Their Place and Fall in Line': The Revisioning of Women's Work in *Herland* and *Emma McChesney & Co.*," *Prospects* 21 (1996): 39–87.

11. Walter Dill Scott, *The Psychology of Advertising* (New York, 1912).

12. Arthur Miller, *Death of a Salesman* (New York: Viking, 1949), 138.

13. Ferber, "Hats Off to the Business Woman!" 6.

14. Ferber, *A Peculiar Treasure,* 15; Gilbert, *Ferber,* 198; Ferber, *A Kind of Magic,* 21.

15. Gilbert, *Ferber,* 424.

16. Ibid., 198–99.

17. Kilmer, "Business Woman Most Domestic," 4.

18. *New York Times,* Apr. 17, 1968, 1.

19. For Ferber's account of the writing of *Cimarron,* see *A Peculiar Treasure,* 324–30.

20. Harry Hansen, rev. of *Cimarron, New York World,* Mar. 20, 1920, 13; Stenley Vestal, rev. of *Cimarron, Saturday Review of Books,* Mar. 22, 1930, 841.

21. Folder 12, box 4, Edna Ferber Collection, State Historical Society of Wisconsin, Madison.

22. *Concordia Blade-Empire,* Apr. 30, 1930, 3, folder 10, box 5, Ferber Collection.

23. Qtd. in Ferber, *A Peculiar Treasure,* 361.

24. Rev. of *Emma McChesney & Co., New York Times,* July 4, 1915, 396.

25. Ferber, *A Peculiar Treasure,* 174.

FOREWORD

Roast Beef, Medium, is not only a food. It is a philosophy.

Seated at Life's Dining Table, with the Menu of Morals before you, your eye wanders a bit over the entrées, the hors d'œuvres, and the things *a la,* though you know that Roast Beef, Medium, is safe, and sane, and sure. It agrees with you. As you hesitate there sounds in your ear a soft and insinuating Voice.

" You'll find the tongue in aspic very nice to-day," purrs the Voice. " May I recommend the chicken pie, country style? Perhaps you'd relish something light and tempting. Eggs Benedictine. Very fine. Or some flaked crab meat, perhaps. With a special Russian sauce."

Roast Beef, Medium! How unimaginative it sounds. How prosaic, and dry! You cast the thought of it aside with the contempt that it deserves, and you assume a fine air of the epicure as you order. There are set before you things encased in pastry; things in frilly paper trousers; things that prick the tongue; sauces

FOREWORD

that pique the palate. There are strange vegetable garnishings, cunningly cut. This is not only Food. These are Viands.

" Everything satisfactory? " inquires the insinuating Voice.

" Yes," you say, and take a hasty sip of water. That paprika has burned your tongue. " Yes. Check, please."

You eye the score, appalled. " Look here! Aren't you over-charging! "

" Our regular price," and you catch a sneer beneath the smugness of the Voice. " It is what every one pays, sir."

You reach deep, deep into your pocket, and you pay. And you rise and go, full but not fed. And later as you take your fifth Moral Pepsin Tablet you say Fool! and Fool! and Fool!

When next we dine we are not tempted by the Voice. We are wary of weird sauces. We shun the cunning aspics. We look about at our neighbor's table. He is eating of things French, and Russian and Hungarian. Of food garnished, and garish and greasy. And with a little sigh of content and resignation we settle down to our Roast Beef, Medium.

E. F.

ROAST BEEF, MEDIUM

ROAST BEEF, MEDIUM

I

ROAST BEEF, MEDIUM

THERE is a journey compared to which the travels of Bunyan's hero were a summer-evening's stroll. The Pilgrims by whom this forced march is taken belong to a maligned fraternity, and are known as traveling men. Sample-case in hand, trunk key in pocket, cigar in mouth, brown derby atilt at an angle of ninety, each young and untried traveler starts on his journey down that road which leads through morasses of chicken *à la* Creole, over greasy mountains of queen fritters made doubly perilous by slippery glaciers of rum sauce, into formidable jungles of breaded veal chops threaded by sanguine and deadly streams of tomato gravy, past sluggish mires of dreadful things *en casserole,* over hills of corned-beef hash, across shaking quagmires of veal glacé, plunging into sloughs of slaw, until, haggard, weary, digestion shattered, complexion gone, he reaches the safe haven of roast beef, medium. Once there, he never again strays, although the pompadoured, white-aproned siren sing-songs in his ear the praises of Irish stew, and pork with apple sauce.

Emma McChesney was eating her solitary supper at the Berger house at Three Rivers, Michigan. She had arrived at the Roast Beef haven many years before. She knew the digestive perils of a small town hotel dining-room as a guide on the snow-covered mountain knows each treacherous pitfall and chasm. Ten years on the road had taught her to recognize the deadly snare that lurks in the seemingly calm bosom of minced chicken with cream sauce. Not for her the impenetrable mysteries of a hamburger and onions. It had been a struggle, brief but terrible, from which Emma McChesney had emerged triumphant, her complexion and figure saved.

No more metaphor. On with the story, which left Emma at her safe and solitary supper.

She had the last number of the *Dry Goods Review* propped up against the vinegar cruet,

and the Worcestershire, and the salt shaker.
Between conscientious, but disinterested mouth-
fuls of medium roast beef, she was reading
the snappy ad set forth by her firm's bitterest
competitors, the Strauss Sans-silk Skirt Company. It was a good reading ad. Emma
McChesney, who had forgotten more about
petticoats than the average skirt salesman ever
knew, presently allowed her luke-warm beef
to grow cold and flabby as she read. Somewhere in her subconscious mind she realized
that the lanky head waitress had placed some
one opposite her at the table. Also, subcon-
sciously, she heard him order liver and bacon,
with onions. She told herself that as soon as
she reached the bottom of the column she'd
look up to see who the fool was. She never
arrived at the column's end.

" I just hate to tear you away from that love
lyric; but if I might trouble you for the vinegar —"

Emma groped for it back of her paper and
shoved it across the table without looking up.

"— and the Worcester —"

One eye on the absorbing column, she passed
the tall bottle. But at its removal her prop

was gone. The *Dry Goods Review* was too weighty for the salt shaker alone.

"— and the salt. Thanks. Warm, isn't it?"

There was a double vertical frown between Emma McChesney's eyes as she glanced up over the top of her *Dry Goods Review*. The frown gave way to a half smile. The glance settled into a stare.

" But then, anybody would have stared. He expected it," she said, afterwards, in telling about it. " I've seen matinée idols, and tailors' supplies salesmen, and Julian Eltinge, but this boy had any male professional beauty I ever saw, looking as handsome and dashing as a bowl of cold oatmeal. And he knew it."

Now, in the ten years that she had been out representing T. A. Buck's Featherloom Petticoats, Emma McChesney had found it necessary to make a rule or two for herself. In the strict observance of one of these she had become past mistress in the fine art of congealing the warm advances of fresh and friendly salesmen of the opposite sex. But this case was different, she told herself. The man across the table was little more than a boy — an amaz-

[4]

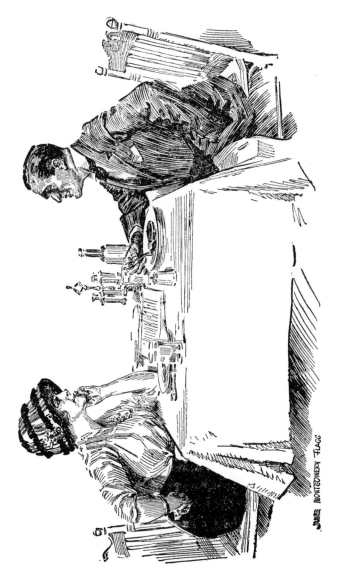

JAMES MONTGOMERY FLAGG

"'Peter Piper picked a peck of pickled peppers,' he announced, glibly"—*Page 7.*

ingly handsome, astonishingly impudent, cock-
ily confident boy, who was staring with inso-
lent approval at Emma McChesney's trim,
shirt-waisted figure, and her fresh, attractive
coloring, and her well-cared-for hair beneath
the smart summer hat.

"It isn't in human nature to be as good-looking as you are," spake Emma McChesney, suddenly, being a person who never trifled with
half-way measures. "I'll bet you have bad
teeth, or an impediment in your speech."

The gorgeous young man smiled. His
teeth were perfect. "Peter Piper picked a
peck of pickled peppers," he announced, glibly.
"Nothing missing there, is there?"

"Must be your morals then," retorted Emma
McChesney. "My! My! And on the road!
Why, the trail of bleeding hearts that you must
leave all the way from Maine to California
would probably make the Red Sea turn white
with envy."

The Fresh Young Kid speared a piece of
liver and looked soulfully up into the adoring
eyes of the waitress who was hovering over him.

"Got any nice hot biscuits to-night, girlie?"
he inquired.

"I'll get you some; sure," wildly promised his handmaiden, and disappeared kitchenward.

"Brand new to the road, aren't you?" observed Emma McChesney, cruelly.

"What makes you think —"

"Liver and bacon, hot biscuits, Worcestershire," elucidated she. "No old-timer would commit suicide that way. After you've been out for two or three years you'll stick to the Rock of Gibraltar — roast beef, medium. Oh, I get wild now and then, and order eggs if the girl says she knows the hen that layed 'em, but plain roast beef, unchloroformed, is the one best bet. You can't go wrong if you stick to it."

The god-like young man leaned forward, forgetting to eat.

"You don't mean to tell me you're on the road!"

"Why not?" demanded Emma McChesney, briskly.

"Oh, fie, fie!" said the handsome youth, throwing her a languishing look. "Any woman as pretty as you are, and with those eyes, and that hair, and figure — Say, Little One, what are you going to do to-night?"

Emma McChesney sugared her tea, and

stirred it, slowly. Then she looked up. " To-
night, you fresh young kid, you! " she said
calmly, " I'm going to dictate two letters,
explaining why business was rotten last week,
and why it's going to pick up next week, and
then I'm going to keep an engagement with a
nine-hour. beauty sleep."

" Don't get sore at a fellow. You'd take
pity on me if you knew how I have to work
to kill an evening in one of these little town-
pump burgs. Kill 'em! It can't be done.
They die harder than the heroine in a ten,
twenty, thirty. From supper to bedtime is
twice as long as from breakfast to supper.
Honest! "

But Emma McChesney looked inexorable,
as women do just before they relent. Said she:
" Oh, I don't know. By the time I get through
trying to convince a bunch of customers that
T. A. Buck's Featherloom Petticoat has every
other skirt in the market looking like a piece of
Fourth of July bunting that's been left out in
the rain, I'm about ready to turn down the
spread and leave a call for six-thirty."

" Be a good fellow," pleaded the unquenchable one. " Let's take in all the nickel shows,

and then see if we can't drown our sorrows in
— er —"

Emma McChesney slipped a coin under her
plate, crumpled her napkin, folded her arms
on the table, and regarded the boy across the
way with what our best talent calls a long,
level look. It was so long and so level that
even the airiness of the buoyant youngster at
whom it was directed began to lessen percepti-
bly, long before Emma began to talk.

" Tell me, young 'un, did, any one ever re-
fuse you anything? I thought not. I should
think that when you realize what you've got to
learn it would scare you to look ahead. I don't
expect you to believe me when I tell you I never
talk to fresh guys like you, but it's true. I
don't know why I'm breaking my rule for you,
unless it's because you're so unbelievably good-
looking that I'm anxious to know where the
blemish is. The Lord don't make 'em perfect,
you know. I'm going to get out those letters,
and then, if it's just the same to you, we'll take
a walk. These nickel shows are getting on
my nerves. It seems to me that if I have to
look at one more Western picture about a fool
girl with her hair in a braid riding a show horse

in the wilds of Clapham Junction and being rescued from a band of almost-Indians by the handsome, but despised Eastern tenderfoot, or if I
see one more of those historical pictures, with
the women wearing costumes that are a pass
between early Egyptian and late State Street, I
know I'll get hysterics and have to be carried
shrieking, up the aisle. Let's walk down Main
Street and look in the store windows, and up
as far as the park and back."

"Great!" assented he. "Is there a park?"

"I don't know," replied Emma McChesney,
"but there is. And for your own good I'm
going to tell you a few things. There's more
to this traveling game than just knocking down
on expenses, talking to every pretty woman you
meet, and learning to ask for fresh white-bread
heels at the Palmer House in Chicago. I'll
meet you in the lobby at eight."

Emma McChesney talked steadily, and
evenly, and generously, from eight until eight-
thirty. She talked from the great storehouse
of practical knowledge which she had accumu-
lated in her ten years on the road. She told
the handsome young cub many things for which
he should have been undyingly thankful. But

when they reached the park — the cool, dim, moon-silvered park, its benches dotted with glimpses of white showing close beside a blur of black, Emma McChesney stopped talking. Not only did she stop talking, but she ceased to think of the boy seated beside her on the bench.

In the band-stand, under the arc-light, in the center of the pretty little square, some neighborhood children were playing a noisy game, with many shrill cries, and much shouting and laughter. Suddenly, from one of the houses across the way, a woman's voice was heard, even above the clamor of the children.

" Fred-dee ! " called the voice. " Maybelle ! Come, now."

And a boy's voice answered, as boys' voices have since Cain was a child playing in the Garden of Eden, and as boys' voices will as long as boys are:

" Aw, ma, I ain't a bit sleepy. We just begun a new game, an' I'm leader. Can't we just stay out a couple of minutes more ? "

" Well, five minutes," agreed the voice. " But don't let me call you again."

Emma McChesney leaned back on the rustic bench and clasped her strong, white hands be-

hind her head, and stared straight ahead into
the soft darkness. And if it had been light you
could have seen that the bitter lines showing
faintly about her mouth were outweighed by the
sweet and gracious light which was glowing in
her eyes.

"Fred-dee!" came the voice of command
again. "May-belle! This minute, now!"

One by one the flying little figures under the
arc-light melted away in the direction of the
commanding voice and home and bed. And
Emma McChesney forgot all about fresh young
kids and featherloom petticoats and discounts
and bills of lading and sample-cases and
grouchy buyers. After all, it had been her
protecting maternal instinct which had been
aroused by the boy at supper, although she had
not known it then. She did not know it now,
for that matter. She was busy remembering
just such evenings in her own life — summer
evenings, filled with the high, shrill laughter of
children at play. She too, had stood in the
doorway, making a funnel of her hands, so
that her clear call through the twilight might
be heard above the cries of the boys and girls.
She had known how loath the little feet had

been to leave their play, and how they had lagged up the porch stairs, and into the house. Years, whose memory she had tried to keep behind her, now suddenly loomed before her in the dim quiet of the little flower-scented park.

A voice broke the silence, and sent her dream-thoughts scattering to the winds.

" Honestly, kid," said the voice, " I could be crazy about you, if you'd let me."

The forgotten figure beside her woke into sudden life. A strong arm encircled her shoulders. A strong hand seized her own, which were clasped behind her head. Two warm, eager lips were pressed upon her lips, checking the little cry of surprise and wrath that rose in her throat.

Emma McChesney wrenched herself free with a violent jerk, and pushed him from her. She did not storm. She did not even rise. She sat very quietly, breathing fast. When she turned at last to look at the boy beside her it seemed that her white profile cut the darkness. The man shrank a little, and would have stammered something, but Emma McChesney checked him.

" You nasty, good-for-nothing, handsome

" 'That was a married kiss—a two-year-old married kiss at
least' "—*Page 17*

young devil, you!" she said. "So you're married."

He sat up with a jerk. "How did you — what makes you think so?"

"That was a married kiss — a two-year-old married kiss, at least. No boy would get as excited as that about kissing an old stager like me. The chances are you're out of practise. I knew that if it wasn't teeth or impediment it must be morals. And it is."

She moved over on the bench until she was close beside him. "Now, listen to me, boy." She leaned forward, impressively. "Are you listening?"

"Yes," answered the handsome young devil, sullenly.

"What I've got to say to you isn't so much for your sake, as for your wife's. I was married when I was eighteen, and stayed married eight years. I've had my divorce ten years, and my boy is seventeen years old. Figure it out. How old is Ann?"

"I don't believe it," he flashed back. "You're not a day over twenty-six — anyway, you don't look it. I —"

"Thanks," drawled Emma. "That's be-

cause you've never seen me in negligée. A
woman's as old as she looks with her hair
on the dresser and bed only a few minutes
away. Do you know why I was decent to you
in the first place? Because I was foolish enough
to think that you reminded me of my own kid.
Every fond mama is gump enough to think
that every Greek god she sees looks like her
own boy, even if her own happens to squint and
have two teeth missing — which mine hasn't,
thank the Lord! He's the greatest young —
Well, now, look here, young 'un. I'm going to
return good for evil. Traveling men and
geniuses should never marry. But as long as
you've done it, you might as well start right.
If you move from this spot till I get through
with you, I'll yell police and murder. Are you
ready? "

"I'm dead sorry, on the square, I am —"

"Ten minutes late," interrupted Emma Mc-
Chesney. "I'm dishing up a sermon, hot, for
one, and you've got to choke it down. Whenever I hear a traveling man howling about his
lonesome evenings, and what a dog's life it is,
and no way for a man to live, I always wonder
what kind of a summer picnic he thinks it is

for his wife. She's really a widow seven
months in the year, without any of a widow's
privileges. Did you ever stop to think what
she's doing evenings? No, you didn't. Well,
I'll tell you. She's sitting home, night after
night, probably embroidering monograms on
your shirt sleeves by way of diversion. And on
Saturday night, which is the night when every
married woman has the inalienable right to be
taken out by her husband, she can listen to the
woman in the flat upstairs getting ready to go
to the theater. The fact that there's a ceiling
between 'em doesn't prevent her from knowing
just where they're going, and why he has
worked himself into a rage over his white lawn
tie, and whether they're taking a taxi or the car
and who they're going to meet afterward at
supper. Just by listening to them coming
downstairs she can tell how much Mrs. Third
Flat's silk stockings cost, and if she's wearing
her new La Valliere or not. Women have that
instinct, you know. Or maybe you don't.
There's so much you've missed."

" Say, look here —" broke from the man beside her. But Emma McChesney laid her cool
fingers on his lips.

[19]

"Nothing from the side-lines, please," she said. "After they've gone she can go to bed, or she can sit up, pretending to read, but really wondering if that squeaky sound coming from the direction of the kitchen is a loose screw in the storm door, or if it's some one trying to break into the flat. And she'd rather sit there, scared green, than go back through that long hall to find out. And when Tillie comes home with her young man at eleven o'clock, though she promised not to stay out later than ten, she rushes back to the kitchen and falls on her neck, she's so happy to see her. Oh, it's a gay life. You talk about the heroism of the early Pilgrim mothers! I'd like to know what they had on the average traveling man's wife."

"Bess goes to the matinée every Saturday," he began, in feeble defense.

"Matinée!" scoffed Emma McChesney. "Do you think any woman goes to matinée by preference? Nobody goes but girls of sixteen, and confirmed old maids without brothers, and traveling men's wives. Matinée! Say, would you ever hesitate to choose between an all-day train and a sleeper? It's the same idea.

ROAST BEEF, MEDIUM

What a woman calls going to the theater is
something very different. It means taking a
nap in the afternoon, so her eyes will be bright
at night, and then starting at about five o'clock
to dress, and lay her husband's clean things out
on the bed. She loves it. She even enjoys
getting his bath towels ready, and putting his
shaving things where he can lay his hands on
'em, and telling the girl to have dinner ready
promptly at six-thirty. It means getting out
her good dress that hangs in the closet with a
cretonne bag covering it, and her black satin
coat, and her hat with the paradise aigrettes
that she bought with what she saved out of the
housekeeping money. It means her best silk
stockings, and her diamond sunburst that he's
going to have made over into a La Valliere just
as soon as business is better. She loves it all,
and her cheeks get pinker and pinker, so that
she really doesn't need the little dash of rouge
that she puts on ' because everybody does it,
don't you know? ' She gets ready, all but her
dress, and then she puts on a kimono and slips
out to the kitchen to make the gravy for the
chicken because the girl never can get it as

smooth as he likes it. That's part of what she calls going to the theater, and having a husband. And if there are children —"

There came a little, inarticulate sound from the boy. But Emma's quick ear caught it.

" No? Well, then, we'll call that one black mark less for you. But if there are children — and for her sake I hope there will be — she's father and mother to them. She brings them up, single-handed, while he's on the road. And the worst she can do is to say to them, ' Just wait until your father gets home. He'll hear of this.' But shucks! When he comes home he can't whip the kids for what they did seven weeks before, and that they've forgotten all about, and for what he never saw, and can't imagine. Besides, he wants his comfort when he gets home. He says he wants a little rest and peace, and he's darned if he's going to run around evenings. Not much, he isn't! But he doesn't object to her making a special effort to cook all those little things that he's been longing for on the road. Oh, there'll be a seat in Heaven for every traveling man's wife — though at that, I'll bet most of 'em will find themselves stuck behind a post."

ROAST BEEF, MEDIUM

" You're all right! " exclaimed Emma Mc-
Chesney's listener, suddenly. " How a woman
like you can waste her time on the road is
more than I can see. And — I want to thank
you. I'm not such a fool —"

" I haven't let you finish a sentence so far,
and I'm not going to yet. Wait a minute.
There's one more paragraph to this sermon.
You remember what I told you about old
stagers, and the roast beef diet? Well, that
applies right through life. It's all very well
to trifle with the little side-dishes at first, but
there comes a time when you've got to quit
fooling with the minced chicken, and the imitation lamb chops of this world, and settle
down to plain, everyday, roast beef, medium.
That other stuff may tickle your palate for a
while, but sooner or later it will turn on you,
and ruin your moral digestion. You stick to
roast beef, medium. It may sound prosaic,
and unimaginative and dry, but you'll find that
it wears in the long run. You can take me
over to the hotel now. I've lost an hour's
sleep, but I don't consider it wasted. And
you'll oblige me by putting the stopper on any
conversation that may occur to you between

here and the hotel. I've talked until I'm so low on words that I'll probably have to sell featherlooms in sign language to-morrow."

They walked to the very doors of the Berger House in silence. But at the foot of the stairs that led to the parlor floor he stopped, and looked into Emma McChesney's face. His own was rather white and tense.

"Look here," he said. "I've got to thank you. That sounds idiotic, but I guess you know what I mean. And I won't ask you to forgive a hound like me. I haven't been so ashamed of myself since I was a kid. Why, if you knew Bess — if you knew —"

"I guess I know Bess, all right. I used to be a Bess, myself. Just because I'm a traveling man it doesn't follow that I've forgotten the Bess feeling. As far as that goes, I don't mind telling you that I've got neuralgia from sitting in that park with my feet in the damp grass. I can feel it in my back teeth, and by eleven o'clock it will be camping over my left eye, with its little brothers doing a war dance up the side of my face. And, boy, I'd give last week's commissions if there was some one to whom I had the right to say: 'Henry, will

"'I won't ask you to forgive a hound like me'"—*Page 24*

you get up and get me a hot-water bag for my neuralgia? It's something awful. And just open the left-hand lower drawer of the chiffonier and get out one of those gauze vests and then get me a safety pin from the tray on my dresser. I'm going to pin it around my head.' "

II

REPRESENTING T. A. BUCK

EMMA McCHESNEY, MRS. (I place it in the background because she generally did) swung off the 2:15, crossed the depot platform, and dived into the hotel 'bus. She had to climb over the feet of a fat man in brown and a lean man in black, to do it. Long practise had made her perfect in the art. She knew that the fat man and the thin man were hogging the end seats so that they could be the first to register and get a choice of rooms when the 'bus reached the hotel. The vehicle smelled of straw, and mold, and stables, and dampness, and tobacco, as 'buses have from old Jonas Chuzzlewit's time to this. Nine years on the road had accustomed Emma McChesney's nostrils to 'bus smells. She gazed stolidly out of the window, crossed one leg over the other, remembered that her snug suit-skirt wasn't built for that attitude,

[28]

uncrossed them again, and caught the delighted and understanding eye of the fat traveling man, who was a symphony in brown — brown suit, brown oxfords, brown scarf, brown hat, brown-bordered handkerchief just peeping over the edge of his pocket. He looked like a colossal chocolate fudge.

" Red-faced, grinning, and a naughty wink — I'll bet he sells coffins and undertakers' supplies," mused Emma McChesney. " And the other one — the tall, lank, funereal affair in black — I suppose his line would be sheet music, or maybe phonographs. Or perhaps he's a lyceum bureau reader, scheduled to give an evening of humorous readings for the Young Men's Sunday Evening Club course at the First M. E. Church."

During those nine years on the road for the Featherloom Skirt Company Emma McChesney had picked up a side line or two on human nature.

She was not surprised to see the fat man in brown and the thin man in black leap out of the 'bus and into the hotel before she had had time to straighten her hat after the wheels had bumped up against the curbing. By the time she reached the desk the two were disappearing in the wake of a bell-boy.

The sartorial triumph behind the desk, languidly read her signature upside down, took a disinterested look at her, and yelled:

" Front! Show the lady up to nineteen."

Emma McChesney took three steps in the direction of the stairway toward which the boy was headed with her bags. Then she stopped.

" Wait a minute, boy," she said, pleasantly enough; and walked back to the desk. She eyed the clerk, a half-smile on her lips, one arm, in its neat tailored sleeve, resting on the marble, while her right forefinger, trimly gloved, tapped an imperative little tattoo. (Perhaps you think that last descriptive sentence is as unnecessary as it is garbled. But don't you get a little picture of her — trim, taut, tailored, mannish-booted, flat-heeled, linen-collared, sailor-hatted?)

" You've made a mistake, haven't you? " she inquired.

" Mistake? " repeated the clerk, removing his eyes from their loving contemplation of his right thumb-nail. " Guess not."

REPRESENTING T. A. BUCK

"Oh, think it over," drawled Emma Mc-
Chesney. "I've never seen nineteen, but I can
describe it with both eyes shut, and one hand
tied behind me. It's an inside room, isn't it,
over the kitchen, and just next to the water butt
where the maids come to draw water for the
scrubbing at 5 A.M.? And the boiler room
gets in its best bumps for nineteen, and the
patent ventilators work just next door, and
there's a pet rat that makes his headquarters in
the wall between eighteen and nineteen, and the
housekeeper whose room is across the hall is
afflicted with a bronchial cough, nights. I'm
wise to the brand of welcome that you fellows
hand out to us women on the road. This is
new territory for me — my first trip West.
Think it over. Don't — er — say, sixty-five
strike you as being nearer my size?"

The clerk stared at Emma McChesney, and
Emma McChesney coolly stared back at the
clerk.

"Our aim," began he, loftily, "is to make
our guests as comfortable as possible on all oc-
casions. But the last lady drummer who —"

"That's all right," interrupted Emma Mc-
Chesney, "but I'm not the kind that steals the

towels, and I don't carry an electric iron with me, either. Also I don't get chummy with the housekeeper and the dining-room girls half an hour after I move in. Most women drummers are living up to their reputations, but some of us are living 'em down. I'm for revision downward. You haven't got my number, that's all."

A slow gleam of unwilling admiration illumined the clerk's chill eye. He turned and extracted another key with its jangling metal tag, from one of the many pigeonholes behind him.

" You win," he said. He leaned over the desk and lowered his voice discreetly. " Say, girlie, go on into the café and have a drink on me."

" Wrong again," answered Emma McChesney. " Never use it. Bad for the complexion. Thanks just the same. Nice little hotel you've got here."

In the corridor leading to sixty-five there was a great litter of pails, and mops, and brooms, and damp rags, and one heard the sigh of a vacuum cleaner.

" Spring house-cleaning," explained the bell-boy, hurdling a pail.

REPRESENTING T. A. BUCK

Emma McChesney picked her way over a little heap of dust-cloths and a ladder or so.

"House-cleaning," she repeated dreamily; "spring house-cleaning." And there came a troubled, yearning light into her eyes. It lingered there after the boy had unlocked and thrown open the door of sixty-five, pocketed his dime, and departed.

Sixty-five was — well, you know what sixty-five generally is in a small Middle-Western town. Iron bed—tan wall-paper — pine table — pine dresser —pine chair — red carpet — stuffy smell —fly buzzing at window — sun beating in from the west. Emma McChesney saw it all in one accustomed glance.

"Lordy, I hate to think what nineteen must be," she told herself, and unclasped her bag. Out came the first aid to the travel-stained — a jar of cold cream. It was followed by powder, chamois, brush, comb, tooth-brush. Emma McChesney dug four fingers into the cold cream jar, slapped the stuff on her face, rubbed it in a bit, wiped it off with a dry towel, straightened her hat, dusted the chamois over her face, glanced at her watch and hurriedly whisked downstairs.

" After all," she mused, " that thin guy might not be out for a music house. Maybe his line is skirts, too. You never can tell. Anyway, I'll beat him to it."

Saturday afternoon and spring-time in a small town! Do you know it? Main Street — on the right side — all a-bustle; farmers' wagons drawn up at the curbing; farmers' wives in the inevitable rusty black with dowdy hats furbished up with a red muslin rose in honor of spring; grand opening at the new five-and-ten-cent store, with women streaming in and streaming out again, each with a souvenir pink carnation pinned to her coat; every one carrying bundles and yellow paper bags that might contain bananas or hats or grass seed; the thirty-two automobiles that the town boasts all dashing up and down the street, driven by hatless youths in careful college clothes; a crowd of at least eleven waiting at Jenson's drug-store corner for the next interurban car.

Emma McChesney found herself strolling when she should have been hustling in the direction of the Novelty Cloak and Suit Store. She was aware of a vague, strangely restless feeling in the region of her heart — or was it her liver? — or her lungs?

Reluctantly she turned in at the entrance of the Novelty Cloak and Suit Store and asked for the buyer. (Here we might introduce one of those side-splitting little business deal scenes. But there can be paid no finer compliment to Emma McChesney's saleswomanship than to state that she landed her man on a busy Saturday afternoon, with a store full of customers and the head woman clerk dead against her from the start.)

As she was leaving:

"Generally it's the other way around," smiled the boss, regarding Emma's trim comeliness, "but seeing you're a lady, why, it'll be on me." He reached for his hat. "Let's go and have — ah — a little something."

"Not any, thanks," Emma McChesney replied, a little wearily.

On her way back to the hotel she frankly loitered. Just to look at her made you certain that she was not of our town. Now, that doesn't imply that the women of our town do not dress well, because they do. But there was something about her — a flirt of chiffon at the throat, or her hat quill stuck in a certain way, or the stitching on her gloves, or the vamp of her shoe — that was of a style which had not reached us yet.

As Emma McChesney loitered, looking in at the shop windows and watching the women hurrying by, intent on the purchase of their Sunday dinners, that vaguely restless feeling seized her again. There were rows of plump fowls in the butcher-shop windows, and juicy roasts. The cunning hand of the butcher had enhanced the redness of the meat by trimmings of curly parsley. Salad things and new vegetables glowed behind the grocers' plate-glass. There were the tender green of lettuces, the coral of tomatoes, the brown-green of stout asparagus stalks, bins of spring peas and beans, and carrots, and bunches of greens for soup. There came over the businesslike soul of Emma McChesney a wild longing to go in and select a ten-pound roast, taking care that there should be just the right proportion of creamy fat and red meat. She wanted to go in and poke her fingers in the ribs of a broiler. She wanted to order wildly of sweet potatoes and vegetables, and soup bones, and apples for pies. She ached to turn back her sleeves and don a blue-and-white checked apron and roll out noodles.

She still was fighting that wild impulse as she walked back to the hotel, went up to her stuffy room, and, without removing hat or coat, seated herself on the edge of the bed and stared long and hard at the tan wall-paper.

There is this peculiarity about tan wall-paper. If you stare at it long enough you begin to see things. Emma McChesney, who pulled down something over thirty-two hundred a year selling Featherloom Petticoats, saw this:

A kitchen, very bright and clean, with a cluttered kind of cleanliness that bespeaks many housewifely tasks under way. There were mixing bowls, and saucepans, and a kettle or so, and from the oven there came the sounds of spluttering and hissing. About the room there hung the divinely delectable scent of freshly baked cookies. Emma McChesney saw herself in an all-enveloping checked gingham apron, her sleeves rolled up, her hair somewhat wild, and one lock powdered with white where she had pushed it back with a floury hand. Her cheeks were surprisingly pink, and her eyes were very bright, and she was scraping a baking board and rolling-pin, and trimming the edges of pie tins, and turning with a whirl to open the oven door, stooping to dip up spoonfuls of gravy only to pour the rich brown liquid over the meat again. There were things on top of the stove that required sticking into with a fork, and other things that demanded tasting and stirring with a spoon. A neighbor came in to borrow a cup of molasses, and Emma urged upon her one of her freshly baked cookies. And there was a ring at the front-door bell, and she had to rush away to do battle with a persistent book agent. . . .

The buzzing fly alighted on Emma McChesney's left eyebrow. She swatted it with a hand that was not quite quick enough, spoiled the picture, and slowly rose from her perch at the bedside.

"Oh, damn!" she remarked, wearily, and went over to the dresser. Then she pulled down her shirtwaist all around and went down to supper.

The dining-room was very warm, and there came a smell of lardy things from the kitchen. Those supping were doing so languidly.

REPRESENTING T. A. BUCK

"I'm dying for something cool, and green, and fresh," remarked Emma to the girl who filled her glass with iced water; "something springish and tempting."

"Well," sing-songed she of the ruffled, starched skirt, "we have ham'n-aigs, mutton chops, cold veal, cold roast —"

"Two, fried," interrupted Emma hopelessly, "and a pot of tea — black."

Supper over she passed through the lobby on her way upstairs. The place was filled with men. They were lolling in the big leather chairs at the window, or standing about, smoking and talking. There was a rattle of dice from the cigar counter, and a burst of laughter from the men gathered about it. It all looked very bright, and cheery, and sociable. Emma McChesney, turning to ascend the stairs to her room, felt that she, too, would like to sit in one of the big leather chairs in the window and talk to some one.

Some one was playing the piano in the parlor. The doors were open. Emma McChesney glanced in. Then she stopped. It was not the appearance of the room that held her. You may have heard of the wilds of an African

[39]

jungle — the trackless wastes of the desert —
the solitude of the forest — the limitless stretch
of the storm-tossed ocean; they are cozy and
snug when compared to the utter and soul-sear-
ing dreariness of a small town hotel parlor.
You know what it is — red carpet, red plush
and brocade furniture, full-length walnut mirror, battered piano on which reposes a sheet of
music given away with the Sunday supplement
of a city paper.

A man was seated at the piano, playing. He
was not playing the Sunday supplement sheet
music. His brown hat was pushed back on his
head and there was a fat cigar in his pursy
mouth, and as he played he squinted up through
the smoke. He was playing Mendelssohn's
Spring Song. Not as you have heard it played
by sweet young things; not as you have heard
it rendered by the Apollo String Quartette.
Under his fingers it was a fragrant, trembling,
laughing, sobbing, exquisite thing. He was
playing it in a way to make you stare straight
ahead and swallow hard.

Emma ·McChesney leaned her head against
the door. The man at the piano did not turn.
So she tip-toed in, found a chair in a corner, and

noiselessly slipped into it. She sat very still, listening, and the past-that-might-have-been, and the future-that-was-to-be, stretched behind and before her, as is strangely often the case when we are listening to music. She stared ahead with eyes that were very wide open and bright. Something in the attitude of the man sitting hunched there over the piano keys, and something in the beauty and pathos of the music brought a hot haze of tears to her eyes. She leaned her head against the back of the chair, and shut her eyes and wept quietly and heart-brokenly. The tears slid down her cheeks, and dropped on her smart tailored waist and her Irish lace jabot, and she didn't care a bit.

The last lovely note died away. The fat man's hands dropped limply to his sides. Emma McChesney stared at them, fascinated. They were quite marvelous hands; not at all the sort òf hands one would expect to see attached to the wrists of a fat man. They were slim, nervous, sensitive hands, pink-tipped, tapering, blue-veined, delicate. As Emma McChesney stared at them the man turned slowly on the revolving stool. His plump, pink face was dolorous, sagging, wan-eyed.

[41]

He watched Emma McChesney as she sat up and dried her eyes. A satisfied light dawned in his face.

"Thanks," he said, and mopped his forehead and chin and neck with the brown-edged handkerchief.

"You — you can't be Paderewski. He's thin. But if he plays any better than that, then I don't want to hear him. You've upset me for the rest of the week. You've started me thinking about things — about things that — that—"

The fat man clasped his thin, nervous hands in front of him and leaned forward.

"About things that you're trying to forget. It starts me that way, too. That's why sometimes I don't touch the keys for weeks. Say, what do you think of a man who can play like that, and who is out on the road for a living just because he knows it's a sure thing? Music! That's my gift. And I've buried it. Why? Because the public won't take a fat man seriously. When he sits down at the piano they begin to howl for Italian rag. Why, I'd rather play the piano in a five-cent moving picture house than do what I'm doing now. But the old man wanted his son to be a business

[42]

man, not a crazy, piano-playing galoot. That's the way he put it. And I was darn fool enough to think he was right. Why can't people stand up and do the things they're out to do! Not one person in a thousand does. Why, take you — I don't know you from Eve, but just from the way you shed the briny I know you're busy regretting."

"Regretting?" repeated Emma McChesney, in a wail. "Do you know what I am? I'm a lady drummer. And do you know what I want to do this minute? I want to clean house. I want to wind a towel around my head, and pin up my skirt, and slosh around with a pail of hot, soapy water. I want to pound a couple of mattresses in the back yard, and eat a cold dinner off the kitchen table. That's what I want to do."

"Well, go on and do it," said the fat man.

"Do it? I haven't any house to clean. I got my divorce ten years ago, and I've been on the road ever since. I don't know why I stick. I'm pulling down a good, fat salary and commissions, but it's no life for a woman, and I know it, but I'm not big enough to quit. It's different with a man on the road. He can spend his evenings taking in two or three nickel shows, or he can stand on the drug-store corner and watch the pretty girls go by, or he can have a game of billiards, or maybe cards. Or he can have a nice, quiet time just going up to his room, and smoking a cigar and writing to his wife or his girl. D'you know what I do?"

"No," answered the fat man, interestedly. "What?"

"Evenings I go up to my room and sew or read. Sew! Every hook and eye and button on my clothes is moored so tight that even the hand laundry can't tear 'em off. You couldn't pry those fastenings away with dynamite. When I find a hole in my stockings I'm tickled to death, because it's something to mend. And read? Everything from the Rules of the House tacked up on the door to spelling out the French short story in the back of the Swell Set Magazine. It's getting on my nerves. Do you know what I do Sunday mornings? No, you don't. Well, I go to church, that's what I do. And I get green with envy watching the other women there getting nervous about 11:45 or so, when the minister is still in knee-deep, and I know they're wondering if Lizzie has basted the chicken often enough, and if she has put the celery in cold water, and the ice-cream is packed in burlap in the cellar, and if she has forgotten to mix in a tablespoon of flour to make it smooth. You can tell by the look on their faces that there's company for dinner. And you know that after dinner they'll sit around, and the men will smoke, and the women folks will go upstairs, and she'll show the other woman her new scalloped, monogrammed, hand-embroidered guest towels, and the waist that her cousin Ethel brought from Paris. And maybe they'll slip off their skirts and lie down on the spare-room bed for a ten minutes' nap. And you can hear the hired girl rattling the dishes in the kitchen, and talking to her lady friend who is helping her wipe up so they can get out early. You can hear the two of them laughing above the clatter of the dishes —"

The fat man banged one fist down on the piano keys with a crash.

" I'm through," he said. " I quit to-night. I've got my own life to live. Here, will you shake on it? I'll quit if you will. You're a born housekeeper. You don't belong on the road any more than I do. It's now or never.

[45]

REPRESENTING T. A. BUCK

And it's going to be now with me. When I
strike the pearly gates I'm not going to have
Saint Peter say to me, ' Ed, old kid, what have
you done with your talents? ' "

" You're right," sobbed Emma McChesney,
her face glowing.

" By the way," interrupted the fat man,
" what's your line? "

" Petticoats. I'm out for T. A. Buck's
Featherloom Skirts. What's yours? "

" Suffering cats! " shouted the fat man.
" D' you mean to tell me that you're the fellow
who sold that bill to Blum, of the Novelty
Cloak and Suit concern, and spoiled a sale for
me? "

" You! Are you —"

" You bet I am. I sell the best little skirt in
the world. Strauss's Sans-silk Petticoat, war-
ranted not to crack, rip, or fall into holes.
Greatest little skirt in the country."

Emma McChesney straightened her collar
and jabot with a jerk, and sat up.

" Oh, now, don't give me that bunk. You've
got a good little seller, all right, but that guar-
anty don't hold water any more than the petticoat contains silk. I know that stuff. It looms

up big in the window displays, but it's got a filler of glucose, or starch or mucilage or something, and two days after you wear it it's as limp as a cheesecloth rag. It's showy, but you take a line like mine, for instance, why —"

"My customers swear by me. I make De-Kalb to-morrow, and there's Nussbaum, of the Paris Emporium, the biggest store there, who just —"

"I make DeKalb, too," remarked Emma McChesney, the light of battle in her eye.

"You mean," gently insinuated the fat man, "that you were going to, but that's all over now."

"Huh?" said Emma.

"Our agreement, you know," the fat man reminded her, sweetly. "You aren't going back on that. The cottage and the Sunday dinner for you, remember."

"Of course," agreed Emma listlessly. "I think I'll go up and get some sleep now. Didn't get much last night on the road."

"Won't you — er — come down and have a little something moist? Or we could have it sent up here," suggested the fat man.

"You're the third man that's asked me that

to-day," snapped Emma McChesney, somewhat crossly. "Say, what do I look like, anyway? I guess I'll have to pin a white ribbon on my coat lapel."

"No offense," put in the fat man, with haste. "I just thought it would bind our bargain. I hope you'll be happy, and contented, and all that, you know."

"Let it go double," replied Emma McChesney, and shook his hand.

"Guess I'll run down and get a smoke," remarked he.

He ran down the stairs in a manner wonderfully airy for one so stout. Emma watched him until he disappeared around a bend in the stairs. Then she walked hastily in the direction of sixty-five.

Down in the lobby the fat man, cigar in mouth, was cautioning the clerk, and emphasizing his remarks with one forefinger.

"I want to leave a call for six-thirty," he was saying. "Not a minute later. I've got to get out of here on that 7:35 for DeKalb. Got a Sunday customer there."

As he turned away a telephone bell tinkled at the desk. The clerk bent his stately head.

" Clerk. Yes, ma'am. No, ma'am, there's no train out of here to-night for DeKalb. To-morrow morning. Seven thirty-five A.M. I sure will. At six-thirty? Surest thing you know."

III

CHICKENS

FOR the benefit of the bewildered reader
it should be said that there are two distinct
species of chickens. There is the chicken which
you find in the barnyard, in the incubator, or on
a hat. And there is the type indigenous to
State Street, Chicago. Each is known by its
feathers. The barnyard variety may puzzle
the amateur fancier, but there is no mistaking
the State Street chicken. It is known by its
soiled, high, white canvas boots; by its tight,
short black skirt; by its slug pearl earrings; by
its bewildering coiffure. By every line of its
slim young body, by every curve of its cheek
and throat you know it is adorably, pitifully
young. By its carmined lip, its near-smart hat,
its babbling of " him," and by the knowledge
which looks boldly out of its eyes you know it is
tragically old.

Seated in the Pullman car, with a friendly

newspaper protecting her bright hair from the doubtful gray-white of the chair cover, Emma McChesney, traveling saleswoman for T. A. Buck's Featherloom Petticoats, was watching the telegraph poles chase each other back to Duluth, Minnesota, and thinking fondly of Mary Cutting, who is the mother-confessor and comforter of the State Street chicken.

Now, Duluth, Minnesota, is trying to be a city. In watching its struggles a hunger for a taste of the real city had come upon Emma Mc-Chesney. She had been out with her late Fall line from May until September. Every Middle-Western town of five thousand inhabitants or over had received its share of Emma McChesney's attention and petticoats. It had been a mystifyingly good season in a bad business year. Even old T. A. himself was almost satisfied. Commissions piled up with gratifying regularity for Emma McChesney. Then, quite suddenly, the lonely evenings, the lack of woman companionship, and the longing for a sight of her seventeen-year-old son had got on Emma McChesney's nerves.

She was two days ahead of her schedule, whereupon she wired her son, thus:

CHICKENS

"Dear Kid:

"Meet me Chicago usual place Friday large time my treat. MOTHER."

Then she had packed her bag, wired Mary Cutting that she would see her Thursday, and had taken the first train out for Chicago.

You might have found the car close, stuffy, and uninteresting. Ten years on the road had taught Emma McChesney to extract a maximum of enjoyment out of a minimum of material. Emma McChesney's favorite occupation was selling T. A. Buck's Featherloom Petticoats, and her favorite pastime was studying men and women. The two things went well together.

When the train stopped for a minute or two you could hear a faint rattle and click from the direction of the smoking compartment where three jewelry salesmen from Providence, Rhode Island, were indulging in their beloved, but dangerous diversion of dice throwing. Just across the aisle was a woman, with her daughter, Chicago-bound to buy a trousseau. They were typical, wealthy small-town women smartly garbed in a fashion not more than twenty minutes late. In the quieter moments of the trip Emma McChesney could hear the mother's high-pitched, East End Ladies' Reading Club voice saying:

" I'd have the velvet suit made fussy, with a real fancy waist to match, for afternoons. You can go anywhere in a handsome velvet three-piece suit."

The girl had smiled, dreamily, and gazed out of the car window. " I wonder," she said, " if there'll be a letter from George. He said he would sit right down and write."

In the safe seclusion of her high-backed chair Emma McChesney smiled approvingly. Seventeen years ago, when her son had been born, and ten years ago, when she had got her divorce, Emma McChesney had thanked her God that her boy had not been a girl. Sometimes, now, she was not so sure about it. It must be fascinating work — selecting velvet suits, made " fussy," for a daughter's trousseau.

Just how fully those five months of small-town existence had got on her nerves Emma McChesney did not realize until the train snorted into the shed and she sniffed the mingled smell of smoke and stockyards and found it sweet in her nostrils. An unholy joy seized her. She entered the Biggest Store and made for the millinery department, yielding to an uncontrollable desire to buy a hat. It was a pert, trim, smart little hat. It made her thirty-six years seem less possible than ever, and her seventeen-year-old son an absurdity.

It was four-thirty when she took the elevator up to Mary Cutting's office on the tenth floor. She knew she would find Mary Cutting there — Mary Cutting, friend, counselor, adviser to every young girl in the great store and to all Chicago's silly, helpless " chickens."

A dragon sat before Mary Cutting's door and wrote names on slips. But at sight of Emma McChesney she laid down her pencil. " Well," smiled the dragon, " you're a sight for sore eyes. There's nobody in there with her. Just walk in and surprise her."

At a rosewood desk in a tiny cozy office sat a pink-cheeked, white-haired woman. You associated her in your mind with black velvet and real lace. She did not look up as Emma McChesney entered. Emma McChesney waited for one small moment. Then:

" Cut out the bank president stuff, Mary

Cutting, and make a fuss over me," she commanded.

The pink-cheeked, white-haired woman looked up. You saw that her eyes were wonderfully young. She made three marks on a piece of paper, pushed a call-button at her desk, rose, and hugged Emma McChesney thoroughly and satisfactorily, then held her off a moment and demanded to know where she had bought her hat.

" Got it ten minutes ago, in the millinery department downstairs. Had to. If I'd have come into New York after five months' exile like this I'd probably have bought a brocade and fur-edged evening wrap, to relieve this feeling of wild joy. For five months I've spent my evenings in my hotel room, or watching the Maude Byrnes Stock Company playing " Lena Rivers," with the ingénue coming out between the acts in a calico apron and a pink sunbonnet and doing a thing they bill as vaudeville. I'm dying to see a real show — a smart one that hasn't run two hundred nights on Broadway — one with pretty girls, and pink tights, and a lot of moonrises, and sunsets and things, and a prima donna in a dress so stun-

[55]

ning that all the women in the audience are busy copying it so they can describe it to their home-dressmaker next day."

"Poor, poor child," said Mary Cutting, "I don't seem to recall any such show."

"Well, it will look that way to me, anyway," said Emma McChesney. "I've wired Jock to meet me to-morrow, and I'm going to give the child a really sizzling little vacation. But to-night you and I will have an old-girl frolic. We'll have dinner together somewhere down-town, and then we'll go to the theater, and after that I'm coming out to that blessed flat of yours and sleep between real sheets. We'll have some sandwiches and beer and other things out of the ice-box, and then we'll have a bathroom bee. We'll let down our back hair, and slap cold cream around, and tell our hearts' secrets and use up all the hot water. Lordy! It will be a luxury to have a bath in a tub that doesn't make you feel as though you wanted to scrub it out with lye and carbolic. Come on, Mary Cutting."

Mary Cutting's pink cheeks dimpled like a girl's.

"You'll never grow up, Emma McChesney

[56]

" 'You'll never grow up, Emma McChesney' "—*Page 56*

— at least, I hope you never will. Sit there in the corner and be a good child, and I'll be ready for you in ten minutes."

Peace settled down on the tiny office. Emma McChesney, there in her corner, surveyed the little room with entire approval. It breathed of things restful, wholesome, comforting. There was a bowl of sweet peas on the desk; there was an Indian sweet grass basket filled with autumn leaves in the corner; there was an air of orderliness and good taste; and there was the pink-cheeked, white-haired woman at the desk.

"There!" said Mary Cutting, at last. She removed her glasses, snapped them up on a little spring-chain near her shoulder, sat back, and smiled upon Emma McChesney.

Emma McChesney smiled back at her. Theirs was not a talking friendship. It was a thing of depth and understanding, like the friendship between two men.

They sat looking into each other's eyes, and down beyond, where the soul holds forth. And because what each saw there was beautiful and sightly they were seized with a shyness such as two men feel when they love each other, and so they awkwardly endeavored to cover up their shyness with words.

" You could stand a facial and a decent scalp massage, Emma," observed Mary Cutting in a tone pregnant with love and devotion. " Your hair looks a little dry. Those small-town manicures don't know how to give a real treatment."

" I'll have it to-morrow morning, before the Kid gets in at eleven. As the Lily Russell of the traveling profession I can't afford to let my beauty wane. That complexion of yours makes me mad, Mary. It goes through a course of hard water and Chicago dirt and comes up looking like a rose leaf with the morning dew on it. Where'll we have supper? "

" I know a new place," replied Mary Cutting. " German, but not greasy."

She was sorting, marking, and pigeonholing various papers and envelopes. When her desk was quite tidy she shut and locked it, and came over to Emma McChesney.

" Something nice happened to me to-day," she said, softly. " Something that made me realize how worth while life is. You know we have five thousand women working here — almost double that during the holidays. A lot of them are under twenty and, Emma, a working girl, under twenty, in a city like this — Well, a brand new girl was looking for me to-day. She didn't know the way to my office, and she didn't know my name. So she stopped one of the older clerks, blushed a little, and said, ' Can you tell me the way to the office of the Comfort Lady? ' That's worth working for, isn't it, Emma McChesney? "

" It's worth living for," answered Emma McChesney, gravely. " It — it's worth dying for. To think that those girls come to you with their little sacred things, their troubles, and misfortunes, and unhappinesses and —"

" And their disgraces — sometimes," Mary Cutting finished for her. " Oh, Emma McChesney, sometimes I wonder why there isn't a national school for the education of mothers. I marvel at their ignorance more and more every day. Remember, Emma, when we were kids our mothers used to send us flying to the grocery on baking day? All the way from our house to Hine's grocery I'd have to keep on saying, over and over: ' Sugar, butter, molasses; sugar, butter, molasses; sugar, butter, molasses.' If I stopped for a minute I'd forget the whole thing. It isn't so different now. Sometimes at night, going home in the car after a day so bad that the whole world seems rotten, I make myself say, over and over, as I used to repeat my ' Sugar, butter, and molasses.' 'It's a glorious, good old world; it's a glorious, good old world; it's a glorious, good old world.' And I daren't stop for a minute for fear of forgetting my lesson."

For the third time in that short half-hour a silence fell between the two — a silence of perfect sympathy and understanding.

Five little strokes, tripping over each other in their haste, came from the tiny clock on Mary Cutting's desk. It roused them both.

" Come on, old girl," said Mary Cutting. " I've a chore or two still to do before my day is finished. Come along, if you like. There's a new girl at the perfumes who wears too many braids, and puffs, and curls, and in the basement misses' ready-to-wear there's another who likes to break store rules about short-sleeved, lace-yoked lingerie waists. And one of the floor managers tells me that a young chap of that callow, semi-objectionable, high-school fraternity, flat-heeled shoe type has been persist-

" 'Well, s'long, then, Shrimp. See you at eight' "—*Page 65*

ently hanging around the desk of the pretty little bundle inspector at the veilings. We're trying to clear the store of that type. They call girls of that description chickens. I wonder why some one hasn't found a name for the masculine chicken."

" I'll give 'em one," said Emma McChesney as they swung down a broad, bright aisle of the store. " Call 'em weasels. That covers their style, occupation, and character."

They swung around the corner to the veilings, and there they saw the very pretty, very blond, very young " chicken " deep in conversation with her weasel. The weasel's trousers were very tight and English, and his hat was properly woolly and Alpine and dented very much on one side and his heels were fashionably flat, and his hair was slickly pompadour.

Mary Cutting and Emma McChesney approached them very quietly just in time to hear the weasel say:

" Well, s' long then, Shrimp. See you at eight."

And he swung around and faced them.

That sick horror of uncertainty which had clutched at Emma McChesney when first she saw the weasel's back held her with awful certainty now. But ten years on the road had taught her self-control, among other things. So she looked steadily and calmly into her son's scarlet face. Jock's father had been a liar.

She put her hand on the boy's arm.

"You're a day ahead of schedule, Jock," she said evenly.

"So are you," retorted Jock, sullenly, his hands jammed into his pockets.

"All the better for both of us, Kid. I was just going over to the hotel to clean up, Jock. Come along, boy."

The boy's jaw set. His eyes sought any haven but that of Emma McChesney's eyes. "I can't," he said, his voice very low. "I've an engagement to take dinner with a bunch of the fellows. We're going down to the Inn. Sorry."

A certain cold rigidity settled over Emma McChesney's face. She eyed her son in silence until his miserable eyes, perforce, looked up into hers.

"I'm afraid you'll have to break your engagement," she said.

She turned to face Mary Cutting's regretful,

understanding gaze. Her eyebrows lifted slightly. Her head inclined ever so little in the direction of the half-scared, half-defiant " chicken."

" You attend to your chicken, Mary," she said. " I'll see to my weasel."

So Emma McChesney and her son Jock, looking remarkably like brother and sister, walked down the broad store aisles and out into the street. There was little conversation between them. When the pillared entrance of the hotel came into sight Jock broke the silence, sullenly:

" Why do you stop at that old barracks? It's a rotten place for a woman. No one stops there but clothing salesmen and boobs who still think it's Chicago's leading hotel. No place for a lady."

" Any place in the world is the place for a lady, Jock," said Emma McChesney quietly.

Automatically she started toward the clerk's desk. Then she remembered, and stopped. " I'll wait here," she said. " Get the key for five-eighteen, will you please? And tell the clerk that I'll want the room adjoining beginning to-night, instead of to-morrow, as I first intended. Tell him you're Mrs. McChesney's son."

He turned away. Emma McChesney brought her handkerchief up to her mouth and held it there a moment, and the skin showed white over the knuckles of her hand. In that moment every one of her thirty-six years were on the table, face up.

"We'll wash up," said Emma McChesney, when he returned, "and then we'll have dinner here."

"I don't want to eat here," objected Jock McChesney. "Besides, there's no reason why I can't keep my evening's engagements."

"And after dinner," went on his mother, as though she had not heard, "we'll get acquainted, Kid."

It was a cheerless, rather tragic meal, though Emma McChesney saw it through from soup to finger-bowls. When it was over she led the way down the old-fashioned, red-carpeted corridors to her room. It was the sort of room to get on its occupant's nerves at any time, with its red plush arm-chairs, its black walnut bed, and its walnut center table inlaid with an apoplectic slab of purplish marble.

" 'I'm still in a position to enforce that ordinance against pouting' "—*Page 71*

CHICKENS

Emma McChesney took off her hat before the dim old mirror, and stood there, fluffing out her hair here, patting it there. Jock had thrown his hat and coat on the bed. He stood now, leaning against the footboard, his legs crossed. his chin on his breast, his whole attitude breathing sullen defiance.

"Jock," said his mother, still patting her hair, "perhaps you don't know it, but you're pouting just as you used to when you wore pinafores. I always hated pouting children. I'd rather hear them howl. I used to spank you for it. I have prided myself on being a modern mother, but I want to mention, in passing, that I'm still in a position to enforce that ordinance against pouting." She turned around abruptly. "Jock, tell me, how did you happen to come here a day ahead of me, and how do you happen to be so chummy with that pretty, weak-faced little thing at the veiling counter, and how, in the name of all that's unbelievable, have you managed to become a grown-up in the last few months?"

Jock regarded the mercifully faded roses in the carpet. His lower lip came forward again.

"Oh, a fellow can't always be tied to his

mother's apron strings. I like to have a little fling myself. I know a lot of fellows here. They are frat brothers. And anyway, I needed some new clothes."

For one long moment Emma McChesney stared, in silence. Then: "Of course," she began, slowly, "I knew you were seventeen years old. I've even bragged about it. I've done more than that — I've gloried in it. But somehow, whenever I thought of you in my heart — and that was a great deal of the time — it was as though you still were a little tyke in knee-pants, with your cap on the back of your head, and a chunk of apple bulging your cheek. Jock, I've been earning close to six thousand a year since I put in that side line of garters. Just how much spending money have I been providing you with?"

Jock twirled a coat button uncomfortably. "Well, quite a lot. But a fellow's got to have money to keep up appearances. A lot of the fellows in my crowd have more than I. There are clothes, and tobacco, and then flowers, and cabs for the skirts — girls, I mean, and —"

"Kid," impressively, "I want you to sit down over there in that plush chair — the red

CHICKENS

one, with the lumps in the back. I want you to be uncomfortable. From where I am sitting I can see that in you there is the making of a first-class cad. That's no pleasant thing for a mother to realize. Now don't interrupt me. I'm going to be chairman, speaker, program, and ways-and-means committee of this meeting. Jock, I got my divorce from your father ten years ago. Now, I'm not going to say anything about him. Just this one thing. You're not going to follow in his footsteps, Kid. Not if I have to take you to pieces like a nickel watch and put you all together again. You're Emma McChesney's son, and ten years from now I intend to be able to brag about it, or I'll want to know the reason why — and it'll have to be a blamed good reason."

"I'd like to know what I've done!" blurted the boy. "Just because I happened to come here a few hours before you expected me, and just because you saw me talking to a girl! Why —"

"It isn't what you've done. It's what those things stand for. I've been at fault. But I'm willing to admit it. Your mother is a working woman, Jock. You don't like that idea,

[73]

do you? But you don't mind spending the money that the working woman provides you with, do you? I'm earning a man's salary. But Jock, you oughtn't to be willing to live on it."

"What do you want me to do?" demanded Jock. "I'm not out of high school yet. Other fellows whose fathers aren't earning as much —"

"Fathers," interrupted Emma McChesney. "There you are. Jock, I don't have to make the distinction for you. You're sufficiently my son to know it, in your heart. I had planned to give you a college education, if you showed yourself deserving. I don't believe in sending a boy in your position to college unless he shows some special leaning toward a profession."

"Mother, you know how wild I am about machines, and motors, and engineering, and all that goes with it. Why I'd work —"

"You'll have to, Jock. That's the only thing that will make a man of you. I've started you wrong, but it isn't too late yet. It's all very well for boys with rich fathers to run to clothes, and city jaunts, and ' chickens,' and cabs and flowers. Your mother is working

[74]

tooth and nail to earn her six thousand, and when you realize just what it means for a woman to battle against men in a man's game, you'll stop being a spender, and become an earner — because you'll want to. I'll tell you what I'm going to do, Kid. I'm going to take you on the road with me for two weeks. You'll learn so many things that at the end of that time the sides of your head will be bulging."

" I'd like it! " exclaimed the boy, sitting up. " It will be regular fun."

" No, it won't," said Emma McChesney; " not after the first three or four days. But it will be worth more to you than a foreign tour and a private tutor."

She came over to him and put her hand on his shoulder. " Your room's just next to mine," she said. " You and I are going to sleep on this. To-morrow we'll have a real day of it, as I promised. If you want to spend it with the fellows, say so. I'm not going to spoil this little lark that I promised you."

" I think," said the boy, looking up into his mother's face, " I think that I'll spend it with you."

The door slammed after him.

[75]

CHICKENS

Emma McChesney remained standing there, in the center of the room. She raised her arms and passed a hand over her forehead and across her hair until it rested on the glossy knot at the back of her head. It was the weary little gesture of a weary, heart-sick woman.

There came a ring at the 'phone.

Emma McChesney crossed the room and picked up the receiver.

"Hello, Mary Cutting," she said, without waiting for the voice at the other end. "What? Oh, I just knew. No, it's all right. I've had some high-class little theatricals of my own, right here, with me in the rôles of leading lady, ingénue, villainess, star, and heavy mother. I've got Mrs. Fiske looking like a First Reader Room kid that's forgotten her Friday piece. What's that?"

There was no sound in the room but the hollow cackle of the voice at the other end of the wire, many miles away.

Then: "Oh, that's all right, Mary Cutting. I owe you a great big debt of gratitude, bless your pink cheeks and white hair! And, Mary," she lowered her voice and glanced in the direction of the room next door, "I don't know how a hard, dry sob would go through the 'phone, so I won't try to get it over. But, Mary, it's been 'sugar, butter, and molasses' for me for the last ten minutes, and I'm dead scared to stop for fear I'll forget it. I guess it's 'sugar, butter, and molasses' for me for the rest of the night, Mary Cutting; just as hard and fast as I can say it, 'sugar, butter, molasses.' "

IV

HIS MOTHER'S SON

F ULL?" repeated Emma McChesney (and
if it weren't for the compositor there'd
be an exclamation point after that question
mark).

"Sorry, Mrs. McChesney," said the clerk,
and he actually looked it, "but there's absolutely nothing stirring. We're full up. The
Benevolent Brotherhood of Bisons is holding
its regular annual state convention here.
We're putting up cots in the hall."

Emma McChesney's keen blue eyes glanced
up from their inspection of the little bunch of
mail which had just been handed her. "Well,
pick out a hall with a southern exposure and
set up a cot or so for me," she said, agreeably,
"because I've come to stay. After selling
Featherloom Petticoats on the road for ten years
I don't see myself trailing up and down this
town looking for a place to lay my head. I've

learned this one large, immovable truth, and that is, that a hotel clerk is a hotel clerk. It makes no difference whether he is stuck back of a marble pillar and hidden by a gold vase full of thirty-six-inch American Beauty roses at the Knickerbocker, or setting the late fall fashions for men in Galesburg, Illinois."

By one small degree was the perfect poise of the peerless personage behind the register jarred. But by only one. He was a hotel night clerk.

" It won't do you any good to get sore, Mrs. McChesney," he began, suavely. " Now a man would —"

" But I'm not a man," interrupted Emma McChesney. " I'm only doing a man's work and earning a man's salary and demanding to be treated with as much consideration as you'd show a man."

The personage busied himself mightily with a pen, and a blotter, and sundry papers, as is the manner of personages when annoyed. " I'd like to accommodate you; I'd like to do it."

" Cheer up," said Emma McChesney, " you're going to. I don't mind a little discomfort. Though I want to mention in passing that if there are any lady Bisons present you needn't bank on doubling me up with them. I've had one experience of that kind. It was in Albia, Iowa. I'd sleep in the kitchen range before I'd go through another."

Up went the erstwhile falling poise. "You're badly mistaken, madam. I'm a member of this order myself, and a finer lot of fellows it has never been my pleasure to know."

"Yes, I know," drawled Emma McChesney. "Do you know, the thing that gets me is the inconsistency of it. Along come a lot of boobs who never use a hotel the year around except to loaf in the lobby, and wear out the leather chairs, and use up the matches and toothpicks and get the baseball returns, and immediately you turn away a traveling man who uses a three-dollar-a-day room, with a sample room downstairs for his stuff, who tips every porter and bell-boy in the place, asks for no favors, and who, if you give him a half-way decent cup of coffee for breakfast, will fall in love with the place and boom it all over the country. Half of your Benevolent Bisons are here on the European plan, with a view to pat-

" 'Son!' echoed the clerk, staring"—*Page 83*

ronizing the free-lunch counters or being asked
to take dinner at the home of some local Bison
whose wife has been cooking up on pies, and
chicken salad and veal roast for the last week."

Emma McChesney leaned over the desk a
little, and lowered her voice to the tone of confidence. " Now, I'm not in the habit of making a nuisance of myself like this. I don't get
so chatty as a rule, and I know that I could
jump over to Monmouth and get first-class ac-
commodations there. But just this once I've a
good reason for wanting to make you and myself a little miserable. Y'see, my son is traveling with me this trip."

" Son! " echoed the clerk, staring.

" Thanks. That's what they all do. After
a while I'll begin to believe that there must be
something hauntingly beautiful and girlish about
me or every one wouldn't petrify when I announce that I've a six-foot son attached to my
apron-strings. He looks twenty-one, but he's
seventeen. He thinks the world's rotten because he can't grow one of those fuzzy little
mustaches that the men are cultivating to match
their hats. He's down at the depot now,
straightening out our baggage. Now I want

[83]

to say this before he gets here. He's been out with me just four days. Those four days have been a revelation, an eye-opener, and a series of rude jolts. He used to think that his mother's job consisted of traveling in Pullmans, eating delicate viands turned out by the hotel chefs, and strewing Featherloom Petticoats along the path. I gave him plenty of money, and he got into the habit of looking lightly upon anything more trifling than a five-dollar bill. He's changing his mind by great leaps. I'm prepared to spend the night in the coal cellar if you'll just fix him up — not too comfortably. It'll be a great lesson for him. There he is now. Just coming in. Fuzzy coat and hat and English stick. Hist! As they say on the stage."

The boy crossed the crowded lobby. There was a little worried, annoyed frown between his eyes. He laid a protecting hand on his mother's arm. Emma McChesney was conscious of a little thrill of pride as she realized that he did not have to look up to meet her gaze.

"Look here, Mother, they tell me there's some sort of a convention here, and the town's

[84]

packed. That's what all those banners and things were for. I hope they've got something decent for us here. I came up with a man who said he didn't think there was a hole left to sleep in."

"You don't say!" exclaimed Emma Mc-Chesney, and turned to the clerk. "This is my son, Jock McChesney — Mr. Sims. Is this true?"

"Glad to know you, sir," said Mr. Sims. "Why, yes, I'm afraid we are pretty well filled up, but seeing it's you maybe we can do something for you."

He ruminated, tapping his teeth with a penholder, and eying the pair before him with a maddening blankness of gaze. Finally:

"I'll do my best, but you can't expect much. I guess I can squeeze another cot into eighty-seven for the young man. There's — let's see now — who's in eighty-seven? Well, there's two Bisons in the double bed, and one in the single, and Fat Ed Meyers in the cot and —"

Emma McChesney stiffened into acute attention. "Meyers?" she interrupted. "Do you mean Ed Meyers of the Strauss Sans-silk Skirt Company?"

"That's so. You two are in the same line, aren't you? He's a great little piano player, Ed is. Ever hear him play?"

"When did he get in?"

"Oh, he just came in fifteen minutes ago on the Ashland division. He's in at supper."

"Oh," said Emma McChesney. The two letters breathed relief.

But relief had no place in the voice, or on the countenance of Jock McChesney. He bristled with belligerence. "This cattle-car style of sleeping don't make a hit. I haven't had a decent night's rest for three nights. I never could sleep on a sleeper. Can't you fix us up better than that?"

"Best I can do."

"But where's mother going? I see you advertise 'three large and commodious steam-heated sample rooms in connection.' I suppose mother's due to sleep on one of the tables there."

"Jock," Emma McChesney reproved him, "Mr. Sims is doing us a great favor. There isn't another hotel in town that would —"

"You're right, there isn't," agreed Mr. Sims. "I guess the young man is new to this

[86]

traveling game. As I said, I'd like to accommodate you, but — Let's see now. Tell you
what I'll do. If I can get the housekeeper to
go over and sleep in the maids' quarters just for
to-night, you can use her room. There you
are! Of course, it's over the kitchen, and there
may be some little noise early in the morning —"

Emma McChesney raised a protesting hand.
" Don't mention it. Just lead me thither.
I'm so tired I could sleep in an excursion special that was switching at Pittsburgh. Jock,
me child, we're in luck. That's twice in the
same place. The first time was when we were
inspired to eat our supper on the diner instead
of waiting until we reached here to take the
leftovers from the Bisons' grazing. I hope
that housekeeper hasn't a picture of her departed husband dangling, life-size, on the wall
at the foot of the bed. But they always have.
Good-night, son. Don't let the Bisons bite you.
I'll be up at seven."

But it was just 6:30 A.M. when Emma Mc-
Chesney turned the little bend in the stairway
that led to the office. The scrub-woman was
still in possession. The cigar-counter girl had

not yet made her appearance. There was about the place a general air of the night before. All but the night clerk. He was as spruce and trim, and alert and smooth-shaven as only a night clerk can be after a night's vigil.

" 'Morning! " Emma McChesney called to him. She wore blue serge, and a smart fall hat. The late autumn morning was not crisper and sunnier than she.

" Good-morning, Mrs. McChesney," returned Mr. Sims, sonorously. " Have a good night's sleep? I hope the kitchen noises didn't wake you."

Emma McChesney paused with her hand on the door. " Kitchen? Oh, no. I could sleep through a vaudeville china-juggling act. But — what an extraordinarily unpleasant-looking man that housekeeper's husband must have been."

That November morning boasted all those qualities which November-morning writers are so prone to bestow upon the month. But the words wine, and sparkle, and sting, and glow, and snap do not seem to cover it. Emma McChesney stood on the bottom step, looking up and down Main Street and breathing in great

[88]

draughts of that unadjectivable air. Her complexion stood the test of the merciless, astrin-
gent morning and came up triumphantly and
healthily firm and pink and smooth. The town
was still asleep. She started to walk briskly
down the bare and ugly Main Street of the little town. In her big, generous heart, and her
keen, alert mind, there were many sensations and
myriad thoughts, but varied and diverse as they
were they all led back to the boy up there in the
stuffy, over-crowded hotel room — the boy
who was learning his lesson.

Half an hour later she reentered the hotel,
her cheeks glowing. Jock was not yet down.
So she ordered and ate her wise and cautious
breakfast of fruit and cereal and toast and coffee, skimming over her morning paper as she
ate. At 7:30 she was back in the lobby, newspaper in hand. The Bisons were already astir.
She seated herself in a deep chair in a quiet
corner, her eyes glancing up over the top of her
paper toward the stairway. At eight o'clock
Jock McChesney came down.

There was nothing of jauntiness about him.
His eyelids were red. His face had the doughy
look of one whose sleep has been brief and

feverish. As he came toward his mother you noticed a stain on his coat, and a sunburst of wrinkles across one leg of his modish brown trousers.

"Good-morning, son!" said Emma McChesney. "Was it as bad as that?"

Jock McChesney's long fingers curled into a fist.

"Say," he began, his tone venomous, "do you know what those — those — those —"

"Say it!" commanded Emma McChesney. "I'm only your mother. If you keep that in your system your breakfast will curdle in your stomach."

Jock McChesney said it. I know no phrase better fitted to describe his tone than that old favorite of the erotic novelties. It was vibrant with passion. It breathed bitterness. It sizzled with savagery. It — Oh, alliteration is useless.

"Well," said Emma McChesney, encouragingly, "go on."

"Well!" gulped Jock McChesney, and glared; "those two double-bedded, bloomin', blasted Bisons came in at twelve, and the single one about fifteen minutes later. They didn't

" 'Well!' gulped Jock, 'those two double-bedded, bloomin' blasted Bisons—' "—*Page 90*

surprise me. There was a herd of about ninety-three of 'em in the hall, all saying good-night to each other, and planning where they'd meet in the morning, and the time, and place and probable weather conditions. For that matter, there were droves of 'em pounding up and down the halls all night. I never saw such restless cattle. If you'll tell me what makes more noise in the middle of the night than the metal disk of a hotel key banging and clanging up against a door, I'd like to know what it is. My three Bisons were all dolled up with fool ribbons and badges and striped paper canes. When they switched on the light I gave a crack imitation of a tired working man trying to get a little sleep. I breathed regularly and heavily, with an occasional moaning snore. But if those two hippopotamus Bisons had been alone on their native plains they couldn't have cared less. They bellowed, and pawed the earth, and threw their shoes around, and yawned, and stretched and discussed their plans for the next day, and reviewed all their doings of that day. Then one of them said something about turning in, and I was so happy I forgot to snore. Just then another key clanged at the door, in walked a fat man in a brown suit and a brown derby, and stuff was off."

"That," said Emma McChesney, "would be Ed Meyers, of the Strauss Sans-silk Skirt Company."

"None other than our hero." Jock's tone had an added acidity. "It took those four about two minutes to get acquainted. In three minutes they had told their real names, and it turned out that Meyers belonged to an organization that was a second cousin of the Bisons. In five minutes they had got together a deck and a pile of chips and were shirt-sleeving it around a game of pinochle. I would doze off to the slap of cards, and the click of chips, and wake up when the bell-boy came in with another round, which he did every six minutes. When I got up this morning I found that Fat Ed Meyers had been sitting on the chair over which I trustingly had draped my trousers. This sunburst of wrinkles is where he mostly sat. This spot on my coat is where a Bison drank his beer."

Emma McChesney folded her paper and rose, smiling. "It is sort of trying, I suppose, if you're not used to it."

"Used to it!" shouted the outraged Jock. "Used to it! Do you mean to tell me there's nothing unusual about —"

"Not a thing. Oh, of course you don't strike a bunch of Bisons every day. But it happens a good many times. The world is full of Ancient Orders and they're everlastingly getting together and drawing up resolutions and electing officers. Don't you think you'd better go in to breakfast before the Bisons begin to forage? I've had mine."

The gloom which had overspread Jock McChesney's face lifted a little. The hungry boy in him was uppermost. "That's so. I'm going to have some wheat cakes, and steak, and eggs, and coffee, and fruit, and toast, and rolls."

"Why slight the fish?" inquired his mother. Then, as he turned toward the dining-room, "I've two letters to get out. Then I'm going down the street to see a customer. I'll be up at the Sulzberg-Stein department store at nine sharp. There's no use trying to see old Sulzberg before ten, but I'll be there, anyway, and so will Ed Meyers, or I'm no skirt salesman. I want you to meet me there. It will do you good to watch how the overripe orders just drop, ker-plunk, into my lap."

Maybe you know Sulzberg & Stein's big store? No? That's because you've always lived in the city. Old Sulzberg sends his buyers to the New York market twice a year, and they need two floor managers on the main floor now. The money those people spend for red and green decorations at Christmas time, and apple-blossoms and pink crêpe paper shades in the spring, must be something awful. Young Stein goes to Chicago to have his clothes made, and old Sulzberg likes to keep the traveling men waiting in the little ante-room outside his private office.

Jock McChesney finished his huge breakfast, strolled over to Sulzberg & Stein's, and inquired his way to the office only to find that his mother was not yet there. There were three men in the little waiting-room. One of them was Fat Ed Meyers. His huge bulk overflowed the spindle-legged chair on which he sat. His brown derby was in his hands. His eyes were on the closed door at the other side of the room. So were the eyes of the other two travelers. Jock took a vacant seat next to Fat Ed Meyers so that he might, in his mind's eye, pick out a particularly choice spot upon which his hard young fist might land — if only he had the chance. Breaking up a man's sleep like that, the great big overgrown mutt!

"What's your line?" said Ed Meyers, suddenly turning toward Jock.

Prompted by some imp — "Skirts," answered Jock. "Ladies' petticoats." ("As if men ever wore 'em!" he giggled inwardly.)

Ed Meyers shifted around in his chair so that he might better stare at this new foe in the field. His little red mouth was open ludicrously.

"Who're you out for?" he demanded next.

There was a look of Emma McChesney on Jock's face. "Why — er — the Union Underskirt and Hosiery Company of Chicago. New concern."

"Must be," ruminated Ed Meyers. "I never heard of 'em, and I know 'em all. You're starting in young, ain't you, kid! Well, it'll never hurt you. You'll learn something new every day. Now me, I —"

In breezed Emma McChesney. Her quick glance rested immediately upon Meyers and the boy. And in that moment some instinct prompted Jock McChesney to shake his head, ever so slightly, and assume a blankness of expression. And Emma McChesney, with that shrewdness which had made her one of the best salesmen on the road, saw, and miraculously understood.

" How do, Mrs. McChesney," grinned Fat Ed Meyers. " You see I beat you to it."

" So I see," smiled Emma, cheerfully. " I was delayed. Just sold a nice little bill to Watkins down the street." She seated herself across the way, and kept her eyes on that closed door.

" Say, kid," Meyers began, in the husky whisper of the fat man, " I'm going to put you wise to something, seeing you're new to this game. See that lady over there? " He nodded discreetly in Emma McChesney's direction.

" Pretty, isn't she? " said Jock, appreciatively.

" Know who she is? "

" Well — I — she does look familiar but —"

" Oh, come now, quit your bluffing. If you'd ever met that dame you'd remember it. Her name's McChesney — Emma McChesney, and she sells T. A. Buck's Featherloom Petticoats. I'll give her her dues; she's the best little salesman on the road. I'll bet that girl could sell a ruffled, accordion-plaited under-skirt to a fat woman who was trying to reduce. She's got the darndest way with her. And at that she's straight, too."

If Ed Meyers had not been gazing so intently into his hat, trying at the same time to look cherubically benign he might have seen a quick and painful scarlet sweep the face of the boy, coupled with a certain tense look of the muscles around the jaw.

"Well, now, look here," he went on, still in a whisper. "We're both skirt men, you and me. Everything's fair in this game. Maybe you don't know it, but when there's a bunch of the boys waiting around to see the head of the store like this, and there happens to be a lady traveler in the crowd, why, it's considered kind of a professional courtesy to let the lady have the first look-in. See? It ain't so often that three people in the same line get together like this. She knows it, and she's sitting on the edge of her chair, waiting to bolt when that door opens, even if she does act like she was hanging on the words of that lady clerk there. The minute it does open a crack she'll jump up and give me a fleeting, grateful smile, and sail in and cop a fat order away from the old man and his skirt buyer. I'm wise. Say, he may be an oyster, but he knows a pretty woman when he sees one. By the time she's through with him he'll have enough petticoats on hand to last him from now until Turkey goes suffrage. Get me?"

"I get you," answered Jock.

"I say, this is business, and good manners be hanged. When a woman breaks into a man's game like this, let her take her chances like a man. Ain't that straight?"

"You've said something," agreed Jock.

"Now, look here, kid. When that door opens I get up. See? And shoot straight for the old man's office. See? Like a duck. See? Say, I may be fat, kid, but I'm what they call light on my feet, and when I see an order getting away from me I can be so fleet that I have Diana looking like old Weston doing a stretch of muddy country road in a coast to coast hike. See? Now you help me out on this and I'll see that you don't suffer for it.

I'll stick in a good word for you, believe me.
You take the word of an old stager like me and
you won't go far —"

The door opened. Simultaneously three
figures sprang into action. Jock had the seat
nearest the door. With marvelous clumsiness
he managed to place himself in Ed Meyers'
path, then reddened, began an apology, stepped
on both of Ed's feet, jabbed his elbow into his
stomach, and dropped his hat. A second later
the door of old Sulzberg's private office closed
upon Emma McChesney's smart, erect, confident figure.

Now, Ed Meyers' hands were peculiar hands
for a fat man. They were tapering, slender,
delicate, blue-veined, temperamental hands.
At this moment, despite his purpling face, and
his staring eyes, they were the most noticeable
thing about him His fingers clawed the empty
air, quivering, vibrant, as though poised to
clutch at Jock's throat.

Then words came. They spluttered from
his lips. They popped like corn kernels in the
heat of his wrath; they tripped over each other;
they exploded.

" You darned kid, you! " he began, with fas-

cinating fluency. " You thousand-legged, dou-
ble-jointed, ox-footed truck horse. Come on
out of here and I'll lick the shine off your shoes,
you blue-eyed babe, you! What did you get
up for, huh? What did you think this was going to be — a flag drill?"

With a whoop of pure joy Jock McChesney
turned and fled.

They dined together at one o'clock, Emma
McChesney and her son Jock. Suddenly Jock
stopped eating. His eyes were on the door.
"There's that fathead now," he said, excitedly.
"The nerve of him! He's coming over here."

Ed Meyers was waddling toward them with
the quick light step of the fat man. His pink,
full-jowled face was glowing. His eyes were
bright as a boy's. He stopped at their table
and paused for one dramatic moment.

" So, me beauty, you two were in cahoots,
huh? That's the second low-down deal you've
handed me. I haven't forgotten that trick you
turned with Nussbaum at DeKalb. Never
mind, little girl. I'll get back at you yet."

He nodded a contemptuous head in Jock's direction. " Carrying a packer?"

Emma McChesney wiped her fingers dain-

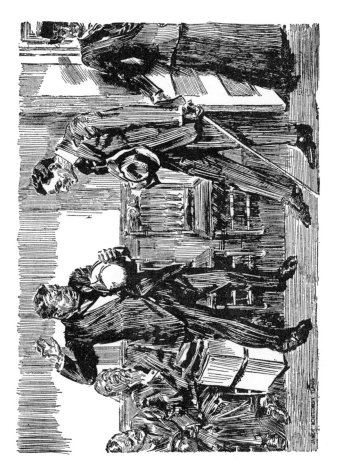

" 'Come on out of here, and I'll lick the shine off your shoes, you blue-eyed babe, you' "—*Page 102*

tily on her napkin, crushed it on the table, and leaned back in her chair. " Men," she observed, wonderingly, " are the cussedest creatures. This chap occupied the same room with you last night and you don't even know his name. Funny! If two strange women had found themselves occupying the same room for a night they wouldn't have got to the kimono and back hair stage before they would not only have known each other's name, but they'd have tried on each other's hats, swapped corset cover patterns, found mutual friends living in Dayton, Ohio, taught each other a new Irish crochet stitch, showed their family photographs, told how their married sister's little girl nearly died with swollen glands, and divided off the mirror into two sections to paste their newly washed handkerchiefs on. Don't tell *me* men have a genius for friendship."

" Well, who is he?" insisted Ed Meyers. " He told me everything but his name this morning. I wish I had throttled him with a bunch of Bisons' badges last night."

" His name," smiled Emma McChesney, " is Jock McChesney. He's my one and only son, and he's put through his first little business deal this morning just to show his mother that he can be a help to his folks if he wants to. Now, Ed Meyers, if you're going to have apoplexy don't you go and have it around this table. My boy is only on his second piece of pie, and I won't have his appetite spoiled."

V

PINK TIGHTS AND GINGHAMS

SOME one — probably one of those French-men whose life job it was to make epigrams — once said that there are but two kinds of women: good women, and bad women. Ever since then problem playwrights have been putting that fiction into the mouths of wronged husbands and building their " big scene " around it. But don't you believe it. There are four kinds: good women, bad women, good bad women, and bad good women. And the worst of these is the last. This should be a story of all four kinds, and when it is finished I defy you to discover which is which.

When the red stuff in the thermometer waxes ambitious, so that fat men stand, bulging-eyed, before it and beginning with the ninety mark count up with a horrible satisfaction — ninety-one — ninety-two — ninety-three — NINETY FOUR! by gosh! and the cinders are filtering into your berth, and even the porter is wandering restlessly up and down the aisle like a black soul in purgatory and a white duck coat, then the thing to do is to don those mercifully few garments which the laxity of sleeping-car etiquette permits, slip out between the green curtains and fare forth in search of draughts, liquid and atmospheric.

At midnight Emma McChesney, inured as she was to sleepers and all their horrors, found her lower eight unbearable. With the bravery of desperation she groped about for her cinder-strewn belongings, donned slippers and kimono, waited until the tortured porter's footsteps had squeaked their way to the far end of the car, then sped up the dim aisle toward the back platform. She wrenched open the door, felt the rush of air, drew in a long, grateful, smoke-steam-dust laden lungful of it, felt the breath of it on spine and chest, sneezed, realized that she would be the victim of a summer cold next day, and, knowing, cared not.

" Great, ain't it?" said a voice in the darkness. (Nay, reader. A woman's voice.)

Emma McChesney was of the non-screaming type. But something inside of her suspended action for the fraction of a second. She peered into the darkness.

" 'J' get scared? " inquired the voice. Its owner lurched forward from the corner in which she had been crouching, into the half-light cast by the vestibule night-globe.

Even as men judge one another by a Masonic emblem, an Elk pin, or the band of a cigar, so do women in sleeping-cars weigh each other according to the rules of the Ancient Order of the Kimono. Seven seconds after Emma McChesney first beheld the negligée that stood revealed in the dim light she had its wearer neatly weighed, marked, listed, docketed and placed.

It was the kind of kimono that is associated with straw-colored hair, and French-heeled shoes, and over-fed dogs at the end of a leash. The Japanese are wrongly accused of having perpetrated it. In pattern it showed bright green flowers-that-never-were sprawling on a purple background. A diamond bar fastened it not too near the throat.

It was one of Emma McChesney's boasts that she was the only living woman who could get off a sleeper at Bay City, Michigan, at 5

A.M., without looking like a Swedish immigrant just dumped at Ellis Island. Traveling had become a science with her, as witness her serviceable dark-blue silk kimono, and her hair in a schoolgirl braid down her back.

The blonde woman cast upon Emma McChesney an admiring eye.

" Gawd, ain't it hot! " she said, sociably.

" I wonder," mused Emma McChesney, " if that porter could be hypnotized into making some lemonade — a pitcherful, with a lot of ice in it, and the cold sweat breaking out all over the glass? "

" Lemonade! " echoed the other, wonder and amusement in her tone. " Are they still usin' it? " She leaned against the door, swaying with the motion of the car, and hugging her plump, bare arms. " Travelin' alone? " she asked.

" Oh, yes," replied Emma McChesney, and decided it was time to go in.

" Lonesome, ain't it, without company? Goin' far? "

" I'm accustomed to it. I travel on business, not pleasure. I'm on the road, representing T. A. Buck's Featherloom Petticoats! "

PINK TIGHTS AND GINGHAMS

The once handsome violet eyes of the plump blonde widened with surprise. Then they narrowed to critical slits.

"On the road! Sellin' goods! And I thought you was only a kid. It's the way your hair's fixed, I suppose. Say, that must be a hard life for a woman — buttin' into a man's game like that."

"Oh, I suppose any work that takes a woman out into the world —" began Emma McChesney vaguely, her hand on the door-knob.

"Sure," agreed the other. "I ought to know. The hotels and time-tables alone are enough to kill. Who do you suppose makes up train schedules? They don't seem to think no respectable train ought to leave anywhere before eleven-fifty P.M., or arrive after six A.M. We played Ottumwa, Iowa, last night, and here we are jumpin' to Illinois."

In surprise Emma McChesney turned at the door for another look at the hair, figure, complexion and kimono.

"Oh, you're an actress! Well, if you think mine is a hard life for a woman, why —"

"Me!" said the green-gold blonde, and

laughed not prettily. " I ain't a woman. I'm a queen of burlesque."

" Burlesque? You mean one of those —" Emma McChesney stopped, her usually deft tongue floundering.

" One of those ' men only ' troupes? You guessed it. I'm Blanche LeHaye, of the Sam Levin Crackerjack Belles. We get into North Bend at six to-morrow morning, and we play there to-morrow night, Sunday." She took a step forward so that her haggard face and artificially tinted hair were very near Emma Mc-Chesney. " Know what I was thinkin' just one second before you come out here? "

" No; what? "

" I was thinkin' what a cinch it would be to just push aside that canvas thing there by the steps and try what the newspaper accounts call ' jumping into the night.' Say, if I'd had on my other lawnjerie I'll bet I'd have done it."

Into Emma McChesney's understanding heart there swept a wave of pity. But she answered lightly: " Is that supposed to be funny? "

The plump blonde yawned. " It depends on your funny bone. Mine's got blunted. I'm the lady that the Irish comedy guy slaps in the face with a bunch of lettuce. Say, there's something about you that makes a person get gabby and tell things. You'd make a swell clairvoyant."

Beneath the comedy of the bleached hair, and the flaccid face, and the bizarre wrapper; behind the coarseness and vulgarity and ignorance, Emma McChesney's keen mental eye saw something decent and clean and beautiful. And something pitiable, and something tragic.

"I guess you'd better come in and get some sleep," said Emma McChesney; and somehow found her hand resting on the woman's shoulder. So they stood, on the swaying, jolting platform. Blanche LeHaye, of the Sam Levin Crackerjack Belles, looked down, askance, at the hand on her shoulder, as at some strange and interesting object.

"Ten years ago," she said, "that would have started me telling the story of my life, with all the tremolo stops on, and the orchestra in tears. Now it only makes me mad."

Emma McChesney's hand seemed to snatch itself away from the woman's shoulder.

"You can't treat me with your life's history. I'm going in."

PINK TIGHTS AND GINGHAMS

"Wait a minute. Don't go away sore, kid. On the square, I guess I liked the feel of· your hand on my arm, like that. Say, I've done the same thing myself to a strange dog that looked up at me, pitiful. You know, the way you reach down, and pat 'm on the head, and say, 'Nice doggie, nice doggie, old fellow,' even if it is a street cur, with a chawed ear, and no tail. They growl and show their teeth, but they like it. A woman — Lordy! there comes the brakeman. Let's beat it. Ain't we the nervy old hens!"

The female of the species as she is found in sleeping-car dressing-rooms had taught Emma McChesney to rise betimes that she might avoid contact with certain frowsy, shapeless beings armed with bottles of milky liquids, and boxes of rosy pastes, and pencils that made arched and inky lines; beings redolent of bitter almond, and violet toilette water; beings in doubtful corsets and green silk petticoats perfect as to accordion-plaited flounce, but showing slits and tatters farther up; beings jealously guarding their ten inches of mirror space and consenting to move for no one; ladies who had come all the way from Texas and who insisted on telling

"'You can't treat me with your life's history. I'm going in'"
—*Page 113*

about it, despite a mouthful of hairpins; doubt-ful sisters who called one dearie and required to be hooked up; distracted mothers with three small children who wiped their hands on your shirt-waist.

So it was that Emma McChesney, hatted and veiled by 5:45, saw the curtains of the berth opposite rent asunder to disclose the rumpled, shapeless figure of Miss Blanche LeHaye. The queen of burlesque bore in her arms a con-glomerate mass of shoes, corset, purple skirt, bag and green-plumed hat. She paused to stare at Emma McChesney's trim, cool preparedness.

"You must have started to dress as soon's you come in last night. I never slep' a wink till just about half a hour ago. I bet I ain't got more than eleven minutes to dress in. Ain't this a scorcher!"

When the train stopped at North Bend, Emma McChesney, on her way out, collided with a vision in a pongee duster, rose-colored chiffon veil, chamois gloves, and plumed hat. Miss Blanche LeHaye had made the most of her eleven minutes. Her baggage attended to, Emma McChesney climbed into a hotel 'bus. It bore no other passengers. From her corner in

[117]

the vehicle she could see the queen of burlesque standing in the center of the depot platform, surrounded by her company. It was a tawdry, miserable, almost tragic group, the men under-sized, be-diamonded, their skulls oddly shaped, their clothes a satire on the fashions for men, their chins unshaven, their loose lips curved contentedly over cigarettes; the women dreadfully unreal with the pitiless light of the early morning sun glaring down on their bedizened faces, their spotted, garish clothes, their run-down heels, their vivid veils, their matted hair. They were quarreling among themselves, and a flame of hate for the moment lighted up those dull, stupid, vicious faces. Blanche LeHaye appeared to be the center about which the strife waged, for suddenly she flung through the shrill group and walked swiftly over to the 'bus and climbed into it heavily. One of the women turned, her face lived beneath the paint, to scream a great oath after her. The 'bus driver climbed into his seat and took up the reins. After a moment's indecision the little group on the platform turned and trailed off down the street, the women sagging under the weight of their bags, the men, for the most part, hurrying on ahead. When the 'bus lurched past them the woman who had screamed the oath after Blanche LeHaye laughed shrilly and made a face, like a naughty child, whereupon the others laughed in falsetto chorus.

A touch of real color showed in Blanche Le-Haye's flabby cheek. " I'll show'm," she snarled. " I'll show'm I ain't no dead one yet. That hussy of a Zella Dacre thinkin' she can get my part away from me when I ain't lookin'. I wised she was gettin' too sweet to me the last week or so, the lyin' sneak. I'll show'm a leadin' lady's a leadin' lady. Let 'em go to their hash hotels. I'm goin' to the real inn in this town just to let 'em know that I got my dignity to keep up, and that I don't have to mix in with scum like that. You see that there? " She pointed at something in the street. Emma McChesney turney to look. The cheap lithographs of the Sam Levin Crackerjack Belles Company glared at one from the bill-boards.

" That's our paper," explained Blanche Le-Haye. " That's me, in the center of the bunch, with the pink reins in my hands, drivin' that four-in-hand of Johnnies. Hot stuff! Just let Dacre try to get it away from me, that's all. I'll show'm."

She sank back into her corner. Her anger left her with the suddenness characteristic of her type.

"Ain't this heat fierce?" she fretted, and closed her eyes.

Now, Emma McChesney was a broad-minded woman The scars that she had received in her ten years' battle with business reminded her to be tender at sight of the wounds of others. But now, as she studied the woman huddled there in the corner, she was conscious of a shuddering disgust of her — of the soiled blouse, of the cheap finery, of the sunken places around the jaw-bone, of the swollen places beneath the eyes, of the thin, carmined lips, of the —

Blanche LeHaye opened her eyes suddenly and caught the look on Emma McChesney's face. Caught it, and comprehended it. Her eyes narrowed, and she laughed shortly.

"Oh, I dunno," drawled Blanche LeHaye. "I wouldn't go's far's that, kid. Say, when I was your age I didn't plan to be no bum burlesquer neither. I was going to be an actress, with a farm on Long Island, like the rest of 'em. Every real actress has got a farm on Long Island, if it's only there in the mind of the press agent. It's a kind of a religion with 'em. I was goin' to build a house on mine that was goin' to be a cross between a California bungalow and the Horticultural Building at the World's Fair. Say, I ain't the worst, kid. There's others outside of my smear, understand, that I wouldn't change places with."

A dozen apologies surged to Emma McChesney's lips just as the driver drew up at the curbing outside the hotel and jumped down to open the door. She found herself hoping that the hotel clerk would not class her with her companion.

At eleven o'clock that morning Emma McChesney unlocked her door and walked down the red-carpeted hotel corridor. She had had two hours of restful sleep. She had bathed, and breakfasted, and donned clean clothes. She had brushed the cinders out of her hair, and manicured. She felt as alert, and cool and refreshed as she looked, which speaks well for her comfort.

PINK TIGHTS AND GINGHAMS

Halfway down the hall a bedroom door stood open. Emma McChesney glanced in. What she saw made her stop. The next moment she would have hurried on, but the figure within called out to her.

Miss Blanche LeHaye had got into her kimono again. She was slumped in a dejected heap in a chair before the window. There was a tray, with a bottle and some glasses on the table by her side.

" Gawd, ain't it hot! " she whined miserably. " Come on in a minute. I left the door open to catch the breeze, but there ain't any. You look like a peach just off the ice. Got a gent friend in town? "

" No," answered Emma McChesney hurriedly, and turned to go.

" Wait a minute," said Blanche LeHaye, sharply, and rose. She slouched over to where Emma McChesney stood and looked up at her sullenly.

" Why! " gasped Emma McChesney, and involuntarily put out her hand, " why — my dear — you've been crying! Is there —"

" No, there ain't. I can bawl, can't I, if I *am* a bum burlesquer? " She put down the squat little glass she had in her hand and stared resentfully at Emma McChesney's cool, fragrant freshness.

"Say," she demanded suddenly, "whatja mean by lookin' at me the way you did this morning, h'm? Whatja mean? You got a nerve turnin' up your nose at me, you have. I'll just bet you ain't no better than you might be, neither. What the —"

Swiftly Emma McChesney crossed the room and closed the door. Then she came back to where Blanche LeHaye stood.

"Now listen to me," she said. "You shed that purple kimono of yours and hustle into some clothes and come along with me. I mean it. Whenever I'm anywhere near this town I make a jump and Sunday here. I've a friend here named Morrissey — Ethel Morrissey — and she's the biggest-hearted, most understanding friend that a woman ever had. She's skirt and suit buyer at Barker & Fisk's here. I have a standing invitation to spend Sunday at her house. She knows I'm coming. I help get dinner if I feel like it, and wash my hair if I want to, and sit out in the back yard, and fool with the dog, and act like a human being for one day.

PINK TIGHTS AND GINGHAMS

After you've been on the road for ten years a
real Sunday dinner in a real home has got
Sherry's flossiest efforts looking like a picnic col-
lation with ants in the pie. You're coming
with me, more for ·my sake than for yours, because the thought of you sitting here, like this,
would sour the day for me."

Blanche LeHaye's fingers were picking at the
pin which fastened her gown. She smiled, uncertainly.

"What's your game?" she inquired.

"I'll wait for you downstairs," said Emma
McChesney, pleasantly. "Do you ever have
any luck with caramel icing? Ethel's and mine
always curdles."

"Do I?" yelled the queen of burlesque. "I
invented it." And she was down on her knees,
her fingers fumbling with the lock of her suitcase.

Only an Ethel Morrissey, inured to the weird
workings of humanity by years of shrewd skirt
land suit buying, could have stood the test of
having a Blanche LeHaye thrust upon her, an
unexpected guest, and with the woman across
the street sitting on her front porch taking it
all in.

[124]

PINK TIGHTS AND GINGHAMS

At the door — "This is Miss Blanche Le-Haye of the — er — Simon —"

"Sam Levin Crackerjack Belles," put in Miss LeHaye. "Pleased to meet you."

"Come in," said Miss Ethel Morrissey, without batting an eye. "I just 'phoned the hotel. Thought you'd gone back on me, Emma. I'm baking a caramel cake. Don't slam the door. This your first visit here, Miss LeHaye? Excuse me for not shaking hands. I'm all flour. Lay your things in there. Ma's spending the day with Aunt Gus at Forest City and I'm the whole works around here. It's got skirts and suits beat a mile. Hot, ain't it? Say, suppose you girls slip off your waists and I'll give you each an all-over apron that's loose and let's the breeze slide around."

Blanche LeHaye, the garrulous, was strangely silent. When she stepped about it was in the manner of one who is fearful of wakening a sleeper. When she caught the eyes of either of the other women her own glance dropped.

When Ethel Morrissey came in with the blue-and-white gingham aprons Blanche Le-Haye hesitated a long minute before picking

[125]

hers up. Then she held it by both sleeves and looked at it long, and curiously. When she looked up again she found the eyes of the other two upon her. She slipped the apron over her head with a nervous little laugh.

" I've been a pair of pink tights so long," she said, " that I guess I've almost forgotten how to be a woman. But once I get this on I'll bet I can come back."

She proved it from the moment that she measured out the first cupful of brown sugar for the caramel icing. She shed her rings, and pinned her hair back from her forehead, and tucked up her sleeves, and as Emma McChesney watched her a resolve grew in her mind.

The cake disposed of —" Give me some potatoes to peel, will you? " said Blanche LeHaye, suddenly. " Give 'em to me in a brown crock, with a chip out of the side. There's certain things always goes hand-in-hand in your mind. You can't think of one without the other. Now, Lillian Russell and cold cream is one; and new potatoes and brown crocks is another."

She peeled potatoes, sitting hunched up on the kitchen chair with her high heels caught back of the top rung. She chopped spinach un-

JAMES MONTGOMERY FLAGG

"'Now, Lillian Russell and cold cream is one; and new potatoes
and brown crocks is another'"—*Page 126*

til her face was scarlet, and her hair hung in limp strands at the back of her neck. She skinned tomatoes. She scoured pans. She wiped up the white oilcloth table-top with a capable and soapy hand. The heat and bustle of the little kitchen seemed to work some miraculous change in her. Her eyes brightened. Her lips smiled. Once, Emma McChesney and Ethel Morrissey exchanged covert looks when they heard her crooning one of those tuneless chants that women hum when they wring out dishcloths in soapy water.

After dinner, in the cool of the sitting-room, with the shades drawn, and their skirts tucked halfway to their knees, things looked propitious for that first stroke in the plan which had worked itself out in Emma McChesney's alert mind. She caught Blanche LeHaye's eye, and smiled.

"This beats burlesquing, doesn't it?" she said. She leaned forward a bit in her chair. "Tell me, Miss LeHaye, haven't you ever thought of quitting that — the stage — and turning to something — something —"

"Something decent?" Blanche LeHaye finished for her. "I used to. I've got over that.

[129]

Now all I ask is to get a laugh when I kick the comedian's hat off with my toe."

" But there must have been a time —" insinuated Emma McChesney, gently.

Blanche LeHaye grinned broadly at the two women who were watching her so intently.

" I think I ought to tell you," she began, " that I never was a minister's daughter, and I don't remember ever havin' been deserted by my sweetheart when I was young and trusting. If I was to draw a picture of my life it would look like one of those charts that the weather bureau gets out — one of those high and low barometer things, all uphill and downhill like a chain of mountains in a kid's geography."

She shut her eyes and lay back in the depths of the leather-cushioned chair. The three sat in silence for a moment.

" Look here," said Emma McChesney, suddenly, rising and coming over to the woman in the big chair, " that's not the life for a woman like you. I can get you a place in our office — not much, perhaps, but something decent — something to start with. If you —"

" For that matter," put in Ethel Morrissey, quickly, " I could get you something right here in our store. I've been there long enough to have some say-so, and if I recommend you they'd start you in the basement at first, and then, if you made good, they advance you right along."

Blanche LeHaye stood up and, twisting her arm around at the back, began to unbutton her gingham apron.

" I guess you think I'm a bad one, don't you? Well, maybe I am. But I'm not the worst. I've got a brother. He lives out West, and he's rich, and married, and respectable. You know the way a man can climb out of the mud, while a woman just can't wade out of it? Well, that's the way it was with us. His wife's a regular society bug. She wouldn't admit that there was any such truck as me, unless, maybe, the Municipal Protective League, or something, of her town, got to waging a war against burlesque shows. I hadn't seen Len — that's my brother — in years and years. Then one night in Omaha, I glimmed him sitting down in the B. H. row. His face just seemed to rise up at me out of the audience. He recognized me, too. Say, men are all alike. What they see in a dingy, half-fed, ignorant bunch like us, I don't know. But the minute a man goes to Cleveland, or Pittsburgh, or somewhere on business he'll hunt up a burlesque show, and what's more, he'll enjoy it. Funny. Well, Len waited for me after the show, and we had a talk. He told me his troubles, and I told him some of mine, and when we got through I wouldn't have swapped with him. His wife's a wonder. She's climbed to the top of the ladder in her town. And she's pretty, and young-looking, and a regular swell. Len says their home is one of the kind where the rubberneck auto stops while the spieler tells the crowd who lives there, and how he made his money. But they haven't any kids, Len told me. He's crazy about 'em. But his wife don't want any. I wish you could have seen Len's face when he was talking about it."

She dropped the gingham apron in a circle at her feet, and stepped out of it. She walked over to where her own clothes lay in a gaudy heap.

"Exit the gingham. But it's been great." She paused before slipping her skirt over her head. The silence of the other two women seemed to anger her a little.

"I guess you think I'm a bad one, clear through, don't you? Well, I ain't. I don't

" 'Why, girls, I couldn't hold down a job in a candy factory'"
—*Page 135*

hurt anybody but myself. Len's wife — that's what I call bad."

" But I *don't* think you're bad clear through," cried Emma McChesney. " I don't. That's why I made that proposition to you. That's why I want you to get away from all this, and start over again."

" Me? " laughed Blanche LeHaye. " Me! In a office! With ledgers, and sale bills, and accounts, and all that stuff! Why, girls, I couldn't hold down a job in a candy factory. I ain't got any intelligence. I never had. You don't find women with brains in a burlesque troupe. If they had 'em they wouldn't be there. Why, we're the dumbest, most ignorant bunch there is. Most of us are just hired girls, dressed up. That's why you find the Woman's Uplift Union having such a blamed hard time savin' souls. The souls they try to save know just enough to be wise to the fact that they couldn't hold down a five-per-week job. Don't you feel sorry for me. I'm doing the only thing I'm good for."

Emma McChesney put out her hand. " I'm sorry," she said. " I only meant it for —"

" Why, of course," agreed Blanche LeHaye,

heartily. "And you, too." She turned so that her broad, good-natured smile included Ethel Morrissey. "I've had a whale of a time. My fingers are all stained up with new potatoes, and my nails is full of strawberry juice, and I hope it won't come off for a week. And I want to thank you both. I'd like to stay, but I'm going to hump over to the theater. That Dacre's got the nerve to swipe the star's dressing-room if I don't get my trunks in first."

They walked with her to the front porch, making talk as they went. Resentment and discomfiture and a sort of admiration all played across the faces of the two women, whose kindness had met with rebuff. At the foot of the steps Blanche LeHaye, prima donna of the Sam Levin Crackerjack Belles turned.

"Oh, say," she called. "I almost forgot. I want to tell you that if you wait until your caramel is off the stove, and then add your butter, when the stuff's hot, but not boilin', it won't lump so. H'm? Don't mention it."

VI

SIMPLY SKIRTS

THEY may differ on the subjects of cigars, samples, hotels, ball teams and pinochle hands, but two things there are upon which they stand united. Every member of that fraternity which is condemned to a hotel bedroom, or a sleeper berth by night, and chained to a sample case by day agrees in this, first: That it isn't what it used to be. Second: If only they could find an opening for a nice, paying gents' furnishing business in a live little town that wasn't swamped with that kind of thing already they'd buy it and settle down like a white man, by George! and quit this peddling. The missus hates it anyhow; and the kids know the iceman better than they do their own dad.

On the morning that Mrs. Emma McChesney (representing T. A. Buck, Featherloom Petticoats) finished her talk with Miss Hattie Stitch, head of Kiser & Bloch's skirt and suit department, she found herself in a rare mood. She hated her job; she loathed her yellow sample cases; she longed to call Miss Stitch a green-eyed cat; and she wished that she had chosen some easy and pleasant way of earning a living, like doing plain and fancy washing and ironing. Emma McChesney had been selling Feather-loom Petticoats on the road for almost ten years, and she was famed throughout her territory for her sane sunniness, and her love of her work. Which speaks badly for Miss Hattie Stitch.

Miss Hattie Stitch hated Emma McChesney with all the hate that a flat-chested, thin-haired woman has for one who can wear a large thirty-six without one inch of alteration, and a hat that turns sharply away from the face. For forty-six weeks in the year Miss Stitch existed in Kiser & Bloch's store at River Falls. For six weeks, two in spring, two in fall, and two in mid-winter, Hattie lived in New York, with a capital L. She went there to select the season's newest models (slightly modified for River Falls), but incidentally she took a regular trousseau with her.

All day long Hattie picked skirt and suit models with unerring good taste and business

judgment. At night she was a creature transformed. Every house of which Hattie bought
did its duty like a soldier and a gentleman.
Nightly Hattie powdered her neck and arms,
performed sacred rites over her hair and nails,
donned a gown so complicated that a hotel maid
had to hook her up the back, and was ready for
her evening's escort at eight. There wasn't a
hat in a grill room from one end of the Crooked
Cow-path to the other that was more wildly bar-
baric than Hattie's, even in these sane and simple days when the bird of paradise has become
the national bird. The buyer of suits for a
thriving department store in a hustling little
Middle-Western town isn't to be neglected.
Whenever a show came to River Falls Hattie
would look bored, pass a weary hand over her
glossy coiffure and say: "Oh, yes. Clever little
show. Saw it two winters ago in New York.
This won't be the original company, of course."
The year that Hattie came back wearing a set
of skunk everyone thought it was lynx until Hattie drew attention to what she called the "brown
tone" in it. After that Old Lady Heinz got
her old skunk furs out of the moth balls and
tobacco and newspapers that had preserved

them, and her daughter cut them up into bands
for the bottom of her skirt, and the cuffs of her
coat. When Kiser & Bloch had their fall and
spring openings the town came ostensibly to
see the new styles, but really to gaze at Hattie
in a new confection, undulating up and down the
department, talking with a heavy Eastern ac-
cent about this or that being " smart " or " good
this year," or having " a world of style," and
sort of trailing her toes after her to give a cling-
ing, Grecian line, like pictures of Ethel Barrymore when she was thin. The year that Hattie confided to some one that she was wearing
only scant bloomers beneath her slinky silk the
floor was mobbed, and they had to call in re-
serves from the basement ladies-and-misses-
ready-to-wear.

Miss Stitch came to New York in March.
On the evening of her arrival she dined with
Fat Ed Meyers, of the Strauss Sans-silk Skirt
Company. He informed her that she looked
like a kid, and that that was some classy little
gown, and it wasn't every woman who could
wear that kind of thing and get away with it.
It took a certain style. Hattie smiled, and
hummed off-key to the tune the orchestra was

playing, and Ed told her it was a shame she didn't do something with that voice.

" I have something to tell you," said Hattie. " Just before I left I had a talk with old Kiser. Or rather, he had a talk with me. You know I have pretty much my own way in my department. Pity if I couldn't have. I made it. Well, Kiser wanted to know why I didn't buy Featherlooms. I said we had no call for 'em, and he came back with figures to prove we're losing a good many hundreds a year by not carrying them. He said the Strauss Sans-silk skirt isn't what it used to be. And he's right."

" Oh, say —" objected Ed Meyers.

" It's true," insisted Hattie. " But I couldn't tell him that I didn't buy Featherlooms because McChesney made me tired. Besides, she never entertains me when I'm in New York. Not that I'd go to the theater in the evening with a woman, because I wouldn't, but — Say, listen. Why don't you make a play for her job? As long as I've got to put in a heavy line of Featherlooms you may as well get the benefit of it. You could double your commissions. I'll bet that woman makes her I-don't know-how-many thousands a year."

Ed Meyers' naturally ruddy complexion took on a richer tone, and he dropped his fork hastily. As he gazed at Miss Stitch his glance was not more than half flattering. "How you women do love each other, don't you! You don't. I don't mind telling you my firm's cutting down its road force, and none of us knows who's going to be beheaded next. But — well — a guy wouldn't want to take a job away from a woman — especially a square little trick like McChesney. Of course she's played me a couple of low-down deals and I promised to get back at her, but that's business. But —"

"So's this," interrupted Miss Hattie Stitch. "And I don't know that she is so square. Let me tell you that I heard she's no better than she might be. I have it on good authority that three weeks ago, at the River House, in our town —"

Their heads came close together over the little, rose-shaded restaurant table.

At eleven o'clock next morning Fat Ed Meyers walked into the office of the T. A. Buck Featherloom Petticoat Company and asked to see old T. A.

"He's in Europe," a stenographer informed

him, " spaing, and sprudeling, and badening.
Want to see T. A. Junior? "

" T. A. Junior! " almost shouted Ed Meyers.
" You don't mean to tell me *that* fellow's taken
hold —"

" Believe *me*. That's why Featherlooms
are soaring and Sans-silks are sinking. Nobody would have believed it. T. A. Junior's
got a live wire looking like a stick of licorice.
When they thought old T. A. was going to
die, young T. A. seemed to straighten out all
of a sudden and take hold. It's about time.
He must be almost forty, but he don't show
it. I don't know, he ain't so good-looking,
but he's got swell eyes."

Ed Meyers turned the knob of the door
marked " Private," and entered, smiling. Ed
Meyers had a smile so cherubic that involuntarily you armed yourself against it.

" Hel-lo Buck! " he called jovially. " I
hear that at last you're taking an interest in
skirts — other than on the hoof." And he
offered young T. A. a large, dark cigar with
a fussy-looking band encircling its middle.
Young T. A. looked at it disinterestedly, and
spake, saying:

[143]

" What are you after? "

" Why, I just dropped in —" began Ed Meyers lamely.

" The dropping," observed T. A. Junior, " is bad around here this morning. I have one little formula for all visitors to-day, regardless of whether they're book agents or skirt salesmen. That is, what can I do for you? "

Ed Meyers tucked his cigar neatly into the extreme right corner of his mouth, pushed his brown derby far back on his head, rested his strangely lean hands on his plump knees, and fixed T. A. Junior with a shrewd blue eye.

" That suits me fine," he agreed. " I never was one to beat around the bush. Look here. I know skirts from the draw-string to the ruffle. It's a woman's garment, but a man's line. There's fifty reasons why a woman can't handle it like a man. For one thing the packing cases weigh twenty-five pounds each, and she's as dependent on a packer and a porter as a baby is on its mother. Another is that if a man has to get up to make a train at 4 A.M. he don't require twenty-five minutes to fasten down three sets of garters, and braid his hair, and hook his waist up the back, and miss his train. And he don't have neuralgic headaches. Then, the head of a skirt department in a store is a woman, ten times out of ten. And lemme tell you," he leaned forward earnestly, " a woman don't like to buy of a woman. Don't ask me why. I'm too modest. But it's the truth."

" Well? " said young T. A., with the rising inflection.

" Well," finished Ed Meyers, " I like your stuff. I think it's great. It's a seller, with the right man to push it. I'd like to handle it. And I'll guarantee I could double the returns from your Middle-Western territory."

T. A. Junior had strangely translucent eyes. Their luminous quality had an odd effect upon any one on whom he happened to turn them. He had been scrawling meaningless curlycues on a piece of paper as Ed Meyers talked. Now he put down the pencil, turned, and looked Ed Meyers fairly in the eye.

" You mean you want Mrs. McChesney's territory? " he asked quietly.

" Well, yes, I do," confessed Ed Meyers, without a blush.

Young T. A. swung back to his desk, tore

from the pad before him the piece of paper on which he had been scrawling, crushed it, and tossed it into the wastebasket with an air of finality.

" Take the second elevator down," he said. " The nearest one's out of order."

For a moment Ed Meyers stared, his fat face purpling. " Oh, very well," he said, rising. " I just made you a business proposition, that's all. I thought I was talking to a business man. Now, old T. A.—"

" That'll be about all," observed T. A. Junior, from his desk.

Ed Meyers started toward the door. Then he paused, turned, and came back to his chair. His heavy jaw jutted out threateningly.

" No, it ain't all, either. I didn't want to mention it, and if you'd treated me like a gentleman, I wouldn't have. But I want to say to you that McChesney's giving this firm a black eye. Morals don't figure with a man on the road, but when a woman breaks into this game, she's got to be on the level."

T. A. Junior rose. The blonde stenographer who had made the admiring remark anent his eyes would have appreciated those features now.

SIMPLY SKIRTS

They glowed luminously into Ed Meyers' pale
blue ones until that gentleman dropped his eyelids in confusion. He seemed at a disadvan-
tage in every way, as T. A. Junior's lean, grace-
ful height towered over the fat man's bulk.

"I don't know Mrs. McChesney," said T.
A. Junior. "I haven't even seen her in six
years. My interest in the business is very recent. I do know that my father swears she's
the best salesman he has on the road. Before you go any further I want to tell you that
you'll have to prove what you just implied, so
definitely, and conclusively, and convincingly
that when you finish you'll have an ordinary engineering blue-print looking like a Turner landscape. Begin."

Ed Meyers, still standing, clutched his derby
tightly and began.

"She's a looker, Emma is. And smooth!
As the top of your desk. But she's getting
careless. Now a decent, hard-working, straight
girl like Miss Hattie Stitch, of Kiser & Bloch's,
River Falls, won't buy of her. You'll find you
don't sell that firm. And they buy big, too.
Why, last summer I had it from the clerk of
the hotel in that town that she ran around all

day with a woman named LeHaye — Blanche
LeHaye, of an aggregation of bum burlesquers
called the Sam Levin Crackerjack Belles. And
say, for a whole month there, she had a tough
young kid traveling with her that she called her
son. Oh, she's queering your line, all right.
The days are past when it used to be a signal
for a loud, merry laugh if you mentioned you
were selling goods on the road. It's a fine art,
and a science these days, and the name of T. A.
Buck has always stood for —"

Downstairs a trim, well-dressed, attractive
woman stepped into the elevator and smiled
radiantly upon the elevator man, who had
smiled first.

" Hello, Jake," she said. " What's old in
New York? I haven't been here in three
months. It's good to be back."

" Seems grand t' see you, Mis' McChesney,"
returned Jake. " Well, nothin' much stirrin'.
Whatcha think of the Grand Central? I understand they're going to have a contrivance so
you can stand on a mat in the waiting-room and
wish yourself down to the track an' train that
you're leavin' on. The G'ints have picked a
bunch of shines this season. T. A. Junior's got

a new sixty-power auto. Genevieve — that yella-headed steno — was married last month to Henry, the shipping clerk. My wife pre· sented me with twin girls Monday. Well, thank *you,* Mrs. McChesney. I guess that'll help some."

Emma McChesney swung down the hall and into the big, bright office. She paused at the head.bookkeeper's desk. The head bookkeeper was a woman. Old Man Buck had learned something about the faithfulness of women em- ployees. The head bookkeeper looked up and said some convincing things.

" Thanks," said Emma, in return. " It's mighty good to be here. Is it true that skirts are going to be full in the back? How's busi- ness? T. A. in? "

" Young T. A. is. But I think he's busy just now. You know T. A. Senior isn't back yet. He had a tight squeeze, I guess. Everybody's talking about the way young T. A. took hold. You know he spent years running around Eu- rope, and he made a specialty of first nights, and first editions, and French cars when he did show up here. But now! He's changed the adver- tising, and designing, and cutting departments

around here until there's as much difference between this place now and the place it was three
months ago as there is between a hoop-skirt and
a hobble. He designed one skirt — Here,
Miss Kelly! Just go in and get one of those
embroidery flounce models for Mrs. McChesney. How's that? Honestly, I'd wear it myself."

Emma McChesney held the garment in her
two hands and looked it over critically. Her
eyes narrowed thoughtfully. She looked up
to reply when the door of T. A. Buck's private
office opened, and Ed Meyers walked briskly
out. Emma McChesney put down the skirt
and crossed the office so that she and he met
just in front of the little gate that formed an
entrance along the railing.

Ed Meyers' mouth twisted itself into a smile.
He put out a welcoming hand.

"Why, hello, stranger! When did you
drive in? How's every little thing? I'm
darned if you don't grow prettier and younger
every day of your sweet life."

"Quit Sans-silks?" inquired Mrs. McChesney briefly.

"Why — no, But I was just telling young

T. A. in there that if I could only find a nice, paying little gents' furnishing business in a live little town that wasn't swamped with that kind of thing already I'd buy it, by George! I'm tired of this peddling."

" Sing that," said Emma McChesney. " It might sound better," and marched into the office marked " Private."

T. A. Junior's good-looking back and semi-bald head were toward her as she entered. She noted, approvingly, woman-fashion, that his neck would never lap over the edge of his collar in the back. Then Young T. A. turned about. He gazed at Emma McChesney, his eyebrows raised inquiringly. Emma McChesney's honest blue eyes, with no translucent nonsense about them, gazed straight back at T. A. Junior.

" I'm Mrs. McChesney. I got in half an hour ago. It's been a good little trip, considering business, and politics, and all that. I'm sorry to hear your father's still ill. He and I always talked over things after my long trip."

Young T. A.'s expert eye did not miss a single point, from the tip of Mrs. McChesney's smart spring hat to the toes of her well-shod feet, with full stops for the fit of her tailored

[153]

suit, the freshness of her gloves, the clearness of her healthy pink skin, the wave of her soft, bright hair.

"How do you do, Mrs. McChesney," said Young T. A. emphatically. "Please sit down. It's a good idea — this talking over your trip. There are several little things — now Kiser & Bloch, of River Falls, for instance. We ought to be selling them. The head of their skirt and suit department is named Stitch, isn't she? Now, what would you say of Miss Stitch?"

"Say?" repeated Emma McChesney quickly. "As a woman, or a buyer?"

T. A. Junior thought a minute. "As a woman."

Mrs. McChesney thoughtfully regarded the tips of her neatly gloved hands. Then she looked up. "The kindest and gentlest thing I can say about her is that if she'd let her hair grow out gray maybe her face wouldn't look so hard."

T. A. Junior flung himself back in his chair and threw back his head and laughed at the ceiling.

Then, "How old is your son?" with disconcerting suddenness.

[154]

" Jock's scandalously near eighteen." In her quick mind Emma McChesney was piecing odds and ends together, and shaping the whole to fit Fat Ed Meyers. A little righteous anger was rising within her.

T. A. Junior searched her face with his glowing eyes.

" Does my father know that you have a young man son? Queer you never mentioned it."

" Queer? Maybe. Also, I don't remember ever having mentioned what church my folks belonged to, or where I was born, or whether I like my steak rare or medium, or what my maiden name was, or the size of my shoes, or whether I take my coffee with or without. That's because I don't believe in dragging private and family affairs into the business relation. I think I ought to tell you that on the way in I met Ed Meyers, of the Strauss Sans-silk Skirt Company, coming out. So anything you say won't surprise me."

" You wouldn't be surprised," asked T. A. Junior smoothly, " if I were to say that I'm considering giving a man your territory? "

Emma McChesney's eyes — those eyes that

had seen so much of the world and its ways, and that still could return your gaze so clearly and honestly — widened until they looked so much like those of a hurt child, or a dumb animal that has received a death wound, that young T. A. dropped his gaze in confusion.

Emma McChesney stood up. Her breath came a little quickly. But when she spoke, her voice was low and almost steady.

"If you expect me to beg you for my job, you're mistaken. T. A. Buck's Featherloom Petticoats have been my existence for almost ten years. I've sold Featherlooms six days in the week, and seven when I had a Sunday customer. They've not only been my business and my means of earning a livelihood, they've been my religion, my diversion, my life, my pet pastime. I've lived petticoats, I've talked petticoats, I've sold petticoats, I've dreamed petticoats — why, I've even worn the darned things! And that's more than any man will ever do for you."

Young T. A. rose. He laughed a little laugh of sheer admiration. Admiration shone, too, in those eyes of his which so many women found irresistible. He took a step forward and laid

"I've lived petticoats, I've talked petticoats, I've dreamed petticoats—why, I've even worn the darn things!" —*Page 156*

one well-shaped hand on Emma McChesney's arm. She did not shrink, so he let his hand slip down the neat blue serge sleeve until it reached her snugly gloved hand.

"You're all right!" he said. His voice was very low, and there was a new note in it. "Listen, girlie. I've just bought a new sixty-power machine. Have dinner with me to-night, will you? And we'll take a run out in the country somewhere. It's warm, even for March. I'll bring along a fur coat for you. H'm?"

Mrs. McChesney stood thoughtfully regarding the hand that covered her own. The blue of her eyes and the pink of her cheeks were a marvel to behold.

"It's a shame," she began slowly, "that you're not twenty-five years younger, so that your father could give you the licking you deserve when he comes home. I shouldn't be surprised if he'd do it anyway. The Lord preserve me from these quiet, deep devils with temperamental hands and luminous eyes. Give me one of the bull-necked, red-faced, hoarse-voiced, fresh kind every time. You know what they're going to say, at least, and you're prepared for them. If I were to tell you how the

[159]

hand you're holding is tingling to box your ears you'd marvel that any human being could have that much repression and live. I've heard of this kind of thing, but I didn't know it happened often off the stage and outside of novels. Let's get down to cases. If I let you make love to me, I keep my job. Is that it?"

"Why — no — I — to tell the truth I was only —"

"Don't embarrass yourself. I just want to tell you that before I'd accept your auto ride I'd open a little fancy art goods and needlework store in Menominee, Michigan, and get out the newest things in Hardanger work and Egyptian embroidery. And that's my notion of zero in occupation. Besides, no plain, everyday workingwoman could enjoy herself in your car because her conscience wouldn't let her. She'd be thinking all the time how she was depriving some poor, hard-working chorus girl of her legitimate pastime, and that would spoil everything. The elevator man told me that you had a new motor car, but the news didn't interest me half as much as that of his having new twin girls. Anything with five thousand dollars can have a sixty-power machine, but only an elevator man on eight dollars a week can afford the luxury of twins."

"My dear Mrs. McChesney —"

"Don't," said Emma McChesney sharply. "I couldn't stand much more. I joke, you know, when other women cry. It isn't so wearing."

She turned abruptly and walked toward the door. T. A. Junior overtook her in three long strides, and placed himself directly before her.

"My cue," said Emma McChesney, with a weary brightness, "to say, 'Let me pass, sir!'"

"Please don't," pleaded T. A. Junior. "I'll remember this the rest of my life. I thought I was a statue of modern business methods, but after to-day I'm going to ask the office boy to help me run this thing. If I could only think of some special way to apologize to you —"

"Oh, it's all right," said Emma McChesney indifferently.

"But it isn't! It isn't! You don't understand. That human jellyfish of a Meyers said some things, and I thought I'd be clever and prove them. I can't ask your pardon. There aren't words enough in the language. Why, you're the finest little woman — you're — you'd restore the faith of a cynic who had chronic indigestion. I wish I — Say, let me relieve you of a couple of those small towns that you hate to make, and give you Cleveland and Cincinnati. And let me — Why say, Mrs. McChesney! Please! Don't! This isn't the time to —"

" I can't help it," sobbed Emma McChesney, her two hands before her face. " I'll stop in a minute. There; I'm stopping now. For Heaven's sake, stop patting me on the head! "

" Please don't be so decent to me," entreated T. A. Junior, his fine eyes more luminous than ever. " If only you'd try to get back at me I wouldn't feel so cut up about it."

Emma McChesney looked up at him, a smile shining radiantly through the tears.

" Very well. I'll do it. Just before I came in they showed me that new embroidery flounced model you just designed. Maybe you don't know it, but women wear only one limp petticoat nowadays. And buttoned shoes. The eyelets in that embroidery are just big enough to catch on the top button of a woman's shoe,

"And found himself addressing the backs of the letters on the
door marked 'Private'"—*Page 165*

and tear, and trip her. I ought to have let you make up a couple of million of them, and then watch them come back on your hands. I was going to tell you, anyway, for T. A. Senior's sake. Now I'm doing it for your own."

"For —" began T. A. Junior excitedly. And found himself addressing the backs of the letters on the door marked " Private," as it slammed after the trim, erect figure in blue.

VII

UNDERNEATH THE HIGH-CUT VEST

WE all carry with us into the one-night-stand country called Sleepland, a practical working nightmare that we use again and again, no matter how varied the theme or setting of our dream-drama. Your surgeon, tossing uneasily on his bed, sees himself cutting to remove an appendix, only to discover that that unpopular portion of his patient's anatomy already bobs in alcoholic glee in a bottle on the top shelf of the laboratory of a more alert professional brother. Your civil engineer constructs imaginary bridges which slump and fall as quickly as they are completed. Your stage favorite, in the throes of a post-lobster nightmare, has a horrid vision of herself " resting " in January. But when he who sells goods on the road groans and tosses in the clutches of a dreadful dream, it is, strangely enough, never of canceled orders, maniacal train schedules, lumpy mattresses, or

[166]

rilely cooked food. These everyday things he
accepts with a philosopher's cheerfulness. No
— his nightmare is always a vision of himself,
sick on the road, at a country hotel in the middle
of a Spring season.

On the third day that she looked with more
than ordinary indifference upon hotel and din-
ing-car food Mrs. Emma McChesney, representing the T. A. Buck Featherloom Petticoat
Company, wondered if, perhaps, she did not need
a bottle of bitter tonic. On the fifth day she noticed that there were chills chasing up and down
her spine, and back and forth from legs to
shoulder-blades when other people were wiping
their chins and foreheads with bedraggled-look-
ing handkerchiefs, and demanding to know how
long this heat was going to last, anyway. On
the sixth day she lost all interest in T. A. Buck's
Featherloom Petticoats. And then she knew
that something was seriously wrong. On the
seventh day, when the blonde and nasal waitress
approached her in the dining-room of the little
hotel at Glen Rock, Minnesota, Emma McChesney's mind somehow failed to grasp the mean-
ing of the all too obvious string of questions
which were put to her — questions ending in

the inevitable " Tea, coffee 'r milk? " At that juncture Emma McChesney had looked up into the girl's face in a puzzled, uncomprehending way, had passed one hand dazedly over her hot forehead, and replied, with great earnestness:

" Yours of the twelfth at hand and contents noted . . . the greatest little skirt on the market . . . he's going to be a son to be proud of, God bless him . . . want to leave a call for seven sharp —"

The lank waitress's face took on an added blankness. One of the two traveling men at the same table started to laugh, but the other put out his hand quickly, rose, and said, " Shut up, you blamed fool! Can't you see the lady's sick? " And started in the direction of her chair.

Even then there came into Emma McChesney's ordinarily well-ordered, alert mind the uncomfortable thought that she was talking nonsense. She made a last effort to order her brain into its usual sane clearness, failed, and saw the coarse white table-cloth rising swiftly and slantingly to meet her head.

It speaks well for Emma McChesney's balance that when she found herself in bed, two

"'Shut up, you blamed fool! Can't you see the lady's sick?'"—*Page 168*

strange women, and one strange man, and an all-too-familiar bell-boy in the room, she did not say, " Where am I? What happened?" Instead she told herself that the amazingly and unbelievably handsome young man bending over her with a stethoscope was a doctor; that the plump, bleached blonde in the white shirtwaist was the hotel housekeeper; that the lank ditto was a waitress; and that the expression on the face of each was that of apprehension, tinged with a pleasurable excitement. So she sat up, dislodging the stethoscope, and ignoring the purpose of the thermometer which had reposed under her tongue.

" Look here!" she said, addressing the doctor in a high, queer voice. " I can't be sick, young man. Haven't time. Not just now. Put it off until August and I'll be as sick as you like. Why, man, this is the middle of June, and I'm due in Minneapolis now."

" Lie down, please," said the handsome young doctor, " and don't dare remove this thermometer again until I tell you to. This can't be put off until August. You're sick right now."

Mrs. McChesney shut her lips over the little

glass tube, and watched the young doctor's impassive face (it takes them no time to learn that trick) and, woman-wise, jumped to her own conclusion.

" How sick? " she demanded, the thermometer read.

" Oh, it won't be so bad," said the very young doctor, with a professionally cheerful smile.

Emma McChesney sat up in bed with a jerk. " You mean — sick! Not ill, or grippy, or run down, but sick! Trained-nurse sick! Hospital sick! Doctor-twice-a-day sick! Table-by-the-bedside-with-bottles-on-it sick! "

" Well — a —" hesitated the doctor, and then took shelter behind a bristling hedge of Latin phrases. Emma McChesney hurdled it at a leap.

" Never mind," she said. " I know." She looked at the faces of those four strangers. Sympathy — real, human sympathy — was uppermost in each. She smiled a faint and friendly little smile at the group. And at that the housekeeper began tucking in the covers at the foot of the bed, and the lank waitress walked to the window and pulled down the shade, and the bell-boy muttered something about ice-water. The doctor patted her wrist lightly and reassuringly.

" You're all awfully good," said Emma Mc-Chesney, her eyes glowing with something other than fever. " I've something to say. It's just this. If I'm going to be sick I'd prefer to be sick right here, unless it's something catching. No hospital. Don't ask me why. I don't know. We people on the road are all alike. Wire T. A. Buck, Junior, of the Featherloom Petticoat Company, New York. You'll find plenty of clean nightgowns in the left-hand tray of my trunk, covered with white tissue paper. Get a nurse that doesn't sniffle, or talk about the palace she nursed in last, where they treated her like a queen and waited on her hand and foot. For goodness' sake, put my switch where nothing will happen to it, and if I die and they run my picture in the *Dry Goods Review* under the caption, ' Veteran Traveling Saleswoman Succumbs at Glen Rock,' I'll haunt the editor." She paused a moment.

" Everything will be all right," said the housekeeper, soothingly. " You'll think you're right at home, it'll be so comfortable. Was there anything else, now? "

UNDERNEATH THE HIGH-CUT VEST

"Yes," said Emma McChesney. "The most important of all. My son, Jock McChesney, is fishing up in the Canadian woods. A telegram may not reach him for three weeks. They're shifting about from camp to camp. Try to get him, but don't scare him too much. You'll find the address under J. in my address book in my handbag. Poor kid. Perhaps it's just as well he doesn't know."

Perhaps it was. At any rate it was true that had the tribe of McChesney been as the leaves of the trees, and had it held a family reunion in Emma McChesney's little hotel bedroom, it would have mattered not at all to her. For she *was* sick — doctor-three-times-a-day-trained-nurse-bottles-by-the-bedside sick, her head, with its bright hair rumpled and dry with the fever, tossing from side to side on the lumpy hotel pillow, or lying terribly silent and inert against the gray-white of the bed linen. She never quite knew how narrowly she escaped that picture in the *Dry Goods Review*.

Then one day the fever began to recede, slowly, whence fevers come, and the indefinable air of suspense and repression that lingers about a sick-room at such a crisis began to lift imper-

ceptibly. There came a time when Emma Mc-
Chesney asked in a weak but sane voice:

" Did Jock come? Did they cut off my
hair?"

"Not yet, dear," the nurse had answered
to the first, " but we'll hear in a day or so, I'm
sure." And, " Your lovely hair! Well, not
if I know it!" to the second.

The spirit of small-town kindliness took
Emma McChesney in its arms. The dingy
little hotel room glowed with flowers. The
story of the sick woman fighting there alone
in the terrors of delirium had gone up and
down about the town. Housewives with a fine
contempt for hotel soups sent broths of chicken
and beef. The local members of the U. C. T.
sent roses enough to tax every vase and wash-
pitcher that the hotel could muster, and asked
their wives to call at the hotel and see what
they could do. The wives came, obediently, but
with suspicion and distrust in their eyes, and remained to pat Emma McChesney's arm, ask to
read aloud to her, and to indulge generally in
that process known as " cheering her up."
Every traveling man who stopped at the little
hotel on his way to Minneapolis added to the

heaped-up offerings at Emma McChesney's shrine. Books and magazines assumed the proportions of a library. One could see the hand of T. A. Buck, Junior, in the cases of mineral water, quarts of wine, cunning cordials and tiny bottles of liqueur that stood in convivial rows on the closet shelf and floor. There came letters, too, and telegrams with such phrases as " let nothing be left undone " and " spare no expense " under T. A. Buck, Junior's, signature.

So Emma McChesney climbed the long, weary hill of illness and pain, reached the top, panting and almost spent, rested there, and began the easy descent on the other side that led to recovery and strength. But something was lacking. That sunny optimism that had been Emma McChesney's most valuable asset was absent. The blue eyes had lost their brave laughter. A despondent droop lingered in the corners of the mouth that had been such a rare mixture of firmness and tenderness. Even the advent of Fat Ed Meyers, her keenest competitor, and representative of the Strauss Sans-silk Company, failed to awaken in her the proper spirit of antagonism. Fat Ed Meyers sent a bunch of violets that devastated the violet beds at the local greenhouse. Emma McChesney regarded them listlessly when the nurse lifted them out of their tissue wrappings. But the name on the card brought a tiny smile to her lips.

"He says he'd like to see you, if you feel able," said Miss Haney, the nurse, when she came up from dinner.

Emma McChesney thought a minute. "Better tell him it's catching," she said.

"He knows it isn't," returned Miss Haney. "But if you don't want him, why —"

"Tell him to come up," interrupted Emma McChesney, suddenly.

A faint gleam of the old humor lighted up her face when Fat Ed Meyers painfully tiptoed in, brown derby in hand, his red face properly doleful, brown shoes squeaking. His figure loomed mountainous in a light-brown summer suit.

"Ain't you ashamed of yourself?" he began, heavily humorous. "Couldn't you find anything better to do in the middle of the season? Say, on the square, girlie, I'm dead sorry. Hard luck, by gosh! Young T. A. himself went out with a line in your territory,

[177]

didn't he? I didn't think that guy had it in him, darned if I did."

"It was sweet of you to send all those violets, Mr. Meyers. I hope you're not disappointed that they couldn't have been worked in the form of a pillow, with 'At Rest' done in white curly-cues."

"Mrs. McChesney!" Ed Meyers' round face expressed righteous reproof, pain, and surprise. "You and I may have had a word, now and then, and I will say that you dealt me a couple of low-down tricks on the road, but that's all in the game. I never held it up against you. Say, nobody ever admired you or appreciated you more than I did —"

"Look out!" said Emma McChesney. "You're speaking in the past tense. Please don't. It makes me nervous."

Ed Meyers laughed, uncomfortably, and glanced yearningly toward the door. He seemed at a loss to account for something he failed to find in the manner and conversation of Mrs. McChesney.

"Son here with you, I suppose," he asked, cheerily, sure that he was on safe ground at last.

[178]

Emma McChesney closed her eyes. The little room became very still. In a panic Ed Meyers looked helplessly from the white face, with its hollow cheeks and closed eyelids to the nurse who sat at the window. That discreet damsel put her finger swiftly to her lips, and shook her head. Ed Meyers rose, hastily, his face a shade redder than usual.

"Well, I guess I gotta be running along. I'm tickled to death to find you looking so fat and sassy. I got an idea you were just stalling for a rest, that's all. Say, Mrs. McChesney, there's a swell little dame in the house named Riordon. She's on the road, too. I don't know what her line is, but she's a friendly kid, with a bunch of talk. A woman always likes to have another woman fussin' around when she's sick. I told her about you, and how I'd bet you'd be crazy to get a chance to talk shop and Featherlooms again. I guess you ain't lost your interest in Featherlooms, eh, what?"

Emma McChesney's face indicated not the faintest knowledge of Featherloom Petticoats. Ed Meyers stared, aghast. And as he stared there came a little knock at the door — a series

[179]

of staccato raps, with feminine knuckles back of them. The nurse went to the door, disapproval on her face. At the turning of the knob there bounced into the room a vision in an Alice-blue suit, plumes to match, pearl earrings, elaborate coiffure of reddish-gold and a complexion that showed an unbelievable trust in the credulity of mankind.

" How-do, dearie! " exclaimed the vision. " You poor kid, you! I heard you was sick, and I says, ' I'm going up to cheer her up if I have to miss my train out to do it.' Say, I was laid up two years ago in Idaho Falls, Idaho, and believe me, I'll never forget it. I don't know how sick I was, but I don't even want to remember how lonesome I was. I just clung to the chamber-maid like she was my own sister. If your nurse wants to go out for an airing I'll sit with you. Glad to."

" That's a grand little idea," agreed Ed Meyers. " I told 'em you'd brighten things up. Well, I'll be going. You'll be as good as new in a week, Mrs. McChesney, don't you worry. So long." And he closed the door after himself with apparent relief.

Miss Haney, the nurse, was already preparing to go out. It was her regular hour for exercise. Mrs. McChesney watched her go with a sinking heart.

" Now! " said Miss Riordon, comfortably, " we girls can have a real, old-fashioned talk. A nurse isn't human. The one I had in Idaho Falls was strictly prophylactic, and antiseptic, and she certainly could give the swell alcohol rubs, but you can't get chummy with a human disinfectant. Your line's skirts, isn't it? "

" Yes."

" Land, I've heard an awful lot about you. The boys on the road certainly speak something grand of you. I'm really jealous. Say, I'd love to show you some of my samples for this season. They're just great. I'll just run down the hall to my room —"

She was gone. Emma McChesney shut her eyes, wearily. Her nerves were twitching. Her thoughts were far, far away from samples and sample cases. So he had turned out to be his worthless father's son after all! He must have got some news of her by now. And he ignored it. He was content to amuse himself up there in the Canadian woods, while his mother —

UNDERNEATH THE HIGH-CUT VEST

Miss Riordon, flushed, and panting a little, burst into the room again, sample-case in hand.

"Lordy, that's heavy! It's a wonder I haven't killed myself before now, wrestling with those blamed things."

Mrs. McChesney sat up on one elbow as Miss Riordon tugged at the sample-case cover. Then she leaned forward, interested in spite of herself at sight of the pile of sheer, white, exquisitely embroidered and lacy garments that lay disclosed as the cover fell back.

"Oh, lingerie! That's an ideal line for a woman. Let's see the yoke in that first nightgown. It's a really wonderful design."

Miss Riordon laughed and shook out the folds of the topmost garment. "Nightgown!" she said, and laughed again. "Take another look."

"Why, what —" began Emma McChesney.

"Shrouds!" announced Miss Riordon complacently.

"Shrouds!" shrieked Mrs. McChesney, and her elbow gave way. She fell back on the pillow.

"Beautiful, ain't they?" Miss Riordon twirled the white garment in her hand.

"They're the very newest thing. You'll notice they're made up slightly hobble, with a French back, and high waist-line in the front. Last season kimono sleeves was all the go, but they're not used this season. This one —"

"Take them away!" screamed Emma McChesney hysterically. "Take them away! Take them away!" And buried her face in her trembling white hands.

Miss Riordon stared. Then she slammed the cover of the case, rose, and started toward the door. But before she reached it, and while the sick woman's sobs were still sounding hysterically the door flew open to admit a tall, slim, miraculously well-dressed young man. The next instant Emma McChesney's lace nightgown was crushed against the top of a correctly high-cut vest, and her tears coursed, unmolested, down the folds of an exquisitely shaded lavender silk necktie.

"Jock!" cried Emma McChesney; and then, "Oh, my son, my son, my beautiful boy!" like a woman in a play.

Jock was holding her tight, and patting her shoulder, and pressing his healthy, glowing cheek close to hers that was so gaunt and pale.

"I got seven wires, all at the same time.
They'd been chasing me for days, up there in
the woods. I thought I'd never get here."

And at that a wonderful thing happened to
Emma McChesney. She lifted her face, and
showed dimples where lines had been, smiles
where tears had coursed, a glow where there
had been a grayish pallor. She leaned back a
bit to survey this son of hers.

"Ugh! how black you are!" It was the
old Emma McChesney that spoke. "You
young devil, you're actually growing a mus-
tache! There's something hard in your left-
hand vest pocket. If it's your fountain pen
you'd better rescue it, because I'm going to
hug you again."

But Jock McChesney was not smiling. He
glanced around the stuffy little hotel room. It
looked stuffier and drearier than ever in contrast with his radiant youth, his glowing freshness, his outdoor tan, his immaculate attire.
He looked at the astonished Miss Riordon.
At his gaze that lady muttered something, and
fled, sample-case banging at her knees. At the
look in his eyes his mother hastened, woman-
wise, to reassure him.

[184]

"At his gaze that lady fled, sample-case banging at her knees"—*Page 184*

"It wasn't so bad, Jock. Now that you're here, it's all right. Jock, I didn't realize just what you meant to me until you didn't come. I didn't realize —"

Jock sat down at the edge of the bed, and slid one arm under his mother's head. There was a grim line about his mouth.

"And I've been fishing," he said. "I've been sprawling under a tree in front of a darned fool stream and wondering whether to fry 'em for lunch now, or to put my hat over my eyes and fall asleep."

His mother reached up and patted his shoulder. But the line around Jock's jaw did not soften. He turned his head to gaze down at his mother.

"Two of those telegrams, and one letter, were from T. A. Buck, Junior," he said. "He met me at Detroit. I never thought I'd stand from a total stranger what I stood from that man."

"Why, what do you mean?" Alarm, dismay, astonishment were in her eyes.

"He said things. And he meant 'em. He showed me, in a perfectly well-bred, cleancut, and most convincing way just what a miserable,

[187]

selfish, low-down, worthless young hound I am."

" He — dared ! —"

" You bet he dared. And then some. And I hadn't an argument to come back with. I don't know just where he got all his information from, but it was straight."

He got up, strode to the window, and came back to the bed. Both hands thrust deep in his pockets, he announced his life plans, thus:

" I'm eighteen years old. And I look twenty-three, and act twenty-five — when I'm with twenty-five-year-olds. I've been as much help and comfort to you as a pet alligator. You've always said that I was to go to college, and I've sort of trained myself to believe I was. Well, I'm not. I want to get into business, with a capital B. And I want to jump in now. This minute. I've started out to be a first-class slob, with you keeping me in pocket money, and clothes, and the Lord knows what all. Why, I —"

" Jock McChesney," said that young man's bewildered mother, " just what did T. A. Buck, Junior, say to you anyway? "

" Plenty. Enough to make me see things.

I used to think that I wanted to get into one of the professions. Professions! You talk about the romance of a civil engineer's life! Why, to be a successful business man these days you've got to be a buccaneer, and a diplomat, and a detective, and a clairvoyant, and an expert mathematician, and a wizard. Business — just plain everyday business — is the gamiest, chanciest, most thrilling line there is to-day, and I'm for it. Let the other guy hang out his shingle and wait for 'em. I'm going out and get mine."

" Any particular line, or just planning to corner the business market generally? " came a cool, not too amused voice from the bed.

" Advertising," replied Jock crisply. " Magazine advertising, to start with. I met a fellow up in the woods — named O'Rourke. He was a star football man at Yale. He's bucking the advertising line now for the *Mastodon Magazine*. He's crazy about it, and says it's the greatest game ever. I want to get into it now — not four years from now."

He stopped abruptly. Emma McChesney regarded him, eyes glowing. Then she gave a happy little laugh, reached for her kimono at the foot of the bed, and prepared to kick off the bedclothes.

" Just run into the hall a second, son," she announced. " I'm going to get up."

" Up! No, you're not! " shouted Jock, making a rush at her. Then, in the exuberance of his splendid young strength, he picked her up, swathed snugly in a roll of sheeting and light blanket, carried her to the big chair by the window, and seated himself, with his surprised and laughing mother in his arms.

But Mrs. McChesney was serious again in a moment. She lay with her head against her boy's breast for a while. Then she spoke what was in her sane, far-seeing mind.

" Jock, if I've ever wished you were a girl, I take it all back now. I'd rather have heard what you just said than any piece of unbelievable good fortune in the world. God bless you for it, dear. But, Jock, you're going to college. No — wait a minute. You'll have a chance to prove the things you just said by getting through in three years instead of the usual four. If you're in earnest you can do it. I want my boy to start into this business war

[190]

"In the exuberance of his young strength, he picked her up"
—*Page 190*

equipped with every means of defense. You called it a game. It's more than that — it's a battle. Compared to the successful business man of to-day the Revolutionary Minute Men were as keen and alert as the Seven Sleepers. I know that there are more non-college men driving street-cars than there are college men. But that doesn't influence me. You could get a job now. Not much of a position, perhaps, but something self-respecting and fairly well-paying. It would teach you many things. You might get a knowledge of human nature that no college could give you. But there's something — poise — self-confidence — assurance — that nothing but college can give you. You will find yourself in those three years. After you finish college you'll have difficulty in fitting into your proper niche, perhaps, and you'll want to curse the day on which you heeded my advice. It'll look as though you had simply wasted those three precious years. But in five or six years after, when your character has jelled, and you've hit your pace, you'll bless me for it. As for a knowledge of humanity, and of business tricks — well, your mother is fairly familiar with the busy marts of trade. If you want to learn folks you can spend your summers selling Featherlooms with me."

"But, mother, you don't understand just why —"

"Yes, dear 'un, I do. After all, remember you're only eighteen. You'll probably spend part of your time rushing around at class proms with a red ribbon in your coat lapel to show you're on the floor committee. And you'll be girl-fussing, too. But you'd be attracted to girls, in or out of college, and I'd rather, just now, that it would be some pretty, nice-thinking college girl in a white sweater and a blue serge skirt, whose worst thought was wondering if you could be cajoled into taking her to the Freshman-Sophomore basketball game, than some red-lipped, black-jet-earringed siren gazing at you across the table in some basement café. And, goodness knows, Jock, you wear your clothes so beautifully that even the haberdashers' salesmen eye you with respect. I've seen 'em. That's one course you needn't take at college."

Jock sat silent, his face grave with thought. "But when I'm earning money — real money

— it's off the road for you," he said, at last. " I don't want this to sound like a scene from East Lynne, but, mother —"

" Um-m-m-m — ye-ee-es," assented Emma McChesney, with no alarming enthusiasm. " Jock dear, carry me back to bed again, will you? And then open the closet door and pull out that big sample-case to the side of my bed. The newest Fall Featherlooms are in it, and somehow, I've just a whimsy notion that I'd like to look 'em over."

VIII

CATCHING UP WITH CHRISTMAS

TEMPTATION himself is not much of a spieler. Raucous-voiced, red-faced, greasy, he stands outside his gaudy tent, dilating on the wonders within. One or two, perhaps, straggle in. But the crowd, made wary by bitter experience of the sham and cheap fraud behind the tawdry canvas flap, stops a moment, laughs, and passes on. Then Temptation, in a panic, seeing his audience drifting away, summons from inside the tent his bespangled and bewitching partner, Mlle. Psychological Moment, the Hypnotic Charmer. She leaps to the platform, bows, pirouettes. The crowd surges toward the ticket-window, nickel in hand.

Six months of bad luck had dogged the footsteps of Mrs. Emma McChesney, traveling

saleswoman for the T. A. Buck Featherloom
Petticoat Company, New York. It had started
with a six-weeks' illness endured in the discom-
fort of a stuffy little hotel bedroom at Glen
Rock, Minnesota. By August she was back in
New York, attending to out-of-town buyers.

Those friendly Middle-Western persons
showed dismay at her pale, hollow-eyed appearance. They spoke to her of teaspoonfuls of
olive-oil taken thrice a day, of mountain air, of
cold baths, and, above all, of the advisability of
leaving the road and taking an inside position.
At that Emma McChesney always showed signs
of unmistakable irritation.

In September her son, Jock McChesney, just
turned eighteen, went blithely off to college, dis-
guised as a millionaire's son in a blue Norfolk,
silk hose, flat-heeled shoes, correctly mounted
walrus bag, and next-week's style in fall hats.
As the train glided out of the great shed Emma
McChesney had waved her handkerchief, smiling like fury and seeing nothing but an indis-
tinct blur as the observation platform slipped
around the curve. She had not felt that same
clutching, desolate sense of loss since the time,

thirteen years before, when she had cut off his curls and watched him march sturdily off to kindergarten.

In October it was plain that spring skirts, instead of being full as predicted, were as scant and plaitless as ever. That spelled gloom for the petticoat business. It was necessary to sell three of the present absurd style to make the profit that had come from the sale of one skirt five years before.

The last week in November, tragedy stalked upon the scene in the death at Marienbad of old T. A. Buck, Mrs. McChesney's stanch friend and beloved employer. Emma McChesney had wept for him as one weeps at the loss of a father.

They had understood each other, those two, from the time that Emma McChesney, divorced, penniless, refusing support from the man she had married eight years before, had found work in the office of the T. A. Buck Featherloom Petticoat Company.

Old Buck had watched her rise from stenographer to head stenographer, from head stenographer to inside saleswoman, from that to a minor road territory, and finally to the position of traveling representative through the coveted Middle-Western territory.

Old T. A. Buck, gruff, grim, direct, far-seeing, kindly, shrewd — he had known Emma McChesney for what she was worth. Once, when she had been disclosing to him a clever business scheme which might be turned into good advertising material, old Buck had slapped his knee with one broad, thick palm and had said:

" Emma McChesney, you ought to have been a man. With that head on a man's shoulders, you could put us out of business."

" I could do it anyway," Mrs. McChesney had retorted.

Old Buck had regarded her a moment over his tortoise-shell rimmed glasses. Then, " I believe you could," he had said, quietly and thoughtfully.

That brings her up to December. To some few millions of people D-e-c-e-m-b-e-r spells Christmas. But to Emma McChesney it spelled the dreaded spring trip. It spelled trains stalled in snowdrifts, baggage delayed, cold hotel bedrooms, harassed, irritable buyers.

It was just six o'clock on the evening of December ninth when Mrs. Emma McChesney swung off the train at Columbus, Ohio, five hours late. As she walked down the broad platform her eyes unconsciously searched the loaded trucks for her own trunks. She'd have recognized them in the hold of a Nile steamer — those grim, travel-scarred sample-trunks. They had a human look to her. She had a way of examining them after each trip, as a fond mother examines her child for stray scratches and bruises when she puts it to bed for the night. She knew each nook and corner of the great trunks as another woman knows her linen-closet or her preserve-shelves.

Columbus, Ohio, was a Featherloom town. Emma McChesney had a fondness for it, with its half rustic, half metropolitan air. Sometimes she likened it to a country girl in a velvet gown, and sometimes to a city girl in white muslin and blue sash. Singer & French always had a Featherloom window twice a year.

The hotel lobby wore a strangely deserted look. December is a slack month for actors and traveling men. Mrs. McChesney registered automatically, received her mail, exchanged greetings with the affable clerk.

CATCHING UP WITH CHRISTMAS

" Send my trunks up to my sample-room as
soon as they get in. Three of 'em — two
sample-trunks and my personal trunk. And I
want to see a porter about putting up some extra
tables. You see, I'm two days late now. I expect two buyers to-morrow morning."

" Send 'em right up, Mrs. McChesney," the
clerk assured her. " Jo'll attend to those
tables. Too bad about old Buck. How's the
skirt business? "

" Skirts? There is no such thing," corrected
Emma McChesney gently. " Sausage-casing
business, you mean."

" Guess you're right, at that. By the way,
how's that handsome youngster of yours? He's
not traveling with you this trip? "

There came a wonderful glow into Emma
McChesney's tired face.

" Jock's at college. Coming home for the
holidays. We're going to have a dizzy week
in New York. I'm wild to see if those three
months of college have done anything to him,
bless his heart! Oh, kind sir, forgive a
mother's fond ravings! Where'd that youngster go with my bag? "

Up at last in the stuffy, unfriendly,

steam-smelling hotel bedroom Emma McChesney prepared to make herself comfortable. A cocky bell-boy switched on the lights, adjusted a shade, straightened a curtain. Mrs. McChesney reached for her pocket-book.

"Just open that window, will you?"

"Pretty cold," remonstrated the bell-boy. "Beginning to snow, too."

"Can't help it. I'll shut it in a minute. The last man that had this room left a dead cigar around somewhere. Send up a waiter, please. I'm going to treat myself to dinner in my room."

The boy gone, she unfastened her collar, loosened a shoe that had pressed a bit too tightly over the instep, took a kimono and toilette articles out of her bag.

"I'll run through my mail," she told herself. "Then I'll get into something loose, see to my trunks, have dinner, and turn in early. Wish Jock were here. We'd have a steak, and some French fried, and a salad, and I'd let the kid make the dressing, even if he does always get in too much vinegar —"

She was glancing through her mail. Two from the firm — one from Mary Cutting —

[202]

one from the Sure-White Laundry at Dayton (hope they found that corset-cover) — one from — why, from Jock! From Jock! And he'd written only two days before. Well!

Sitting there on the edge of the bed she regarded the dear scrawl lovingly, savoring it, as is the way of a woman. Then she took a hairpin from the knot of bright hair (also as is the way of woman) and slit the envelope with a quick, sure rip. M-m-m — it wasn't much as to length. Just a scrawled page. Emma McChesney's eye plunged into it hungrily, a smile of anticipation dimpling her lips, lighting up her face.

"*Dearest Blonde,*" it began.

("The nerve of the young imp!")

He hoped the letter would reach her in time. Knew how this weather mussed up her schedule. He wanted her honest opinion about something — straight, now! One of the frat fellows was giving a Christmas house-party. Awful swells, by the way. He was lucky even to be asked. He'd never remembered a real Christmas — in a home, you know, with a tree, and skating, and regular high jinks, and a dinner that left you feeling like a stuffed gooseberry. Old

CATCHING UP WITH CHRISTMAS

Wells says his grandmother wears lace caps with lavender ribbons. Can you beat it! Of course he felt like a hog, even thinking of wanting to stay away from her at Christmas. Still, Christmas in a New York hotel — ! But the fellows had nagged him to write. Said they'd do it if he didn't. Of course he hated to think of her spending Christmas alone — felt like a bloody villain —

Little by little the smile that had wreathed her lips faded and was gone. The lips still were parted, but by one of those miracles with which the face expresses what is within the heart their expression had changed from pleasure to bitter pain.

She sat there, at the edge of the bed, staring dully until the black scrawls danced on the white page. With the letter before her she raised her hand slowly and wiped away a hot, blinding mist of tears with her open palm. Then she read it again, dully, as though every selfish word of it had not already stamped itself on her brain and heart.

After the second reading she still sat there, her eyes staring down at her lap. Once she brushed an imaginary fleck of lint from the lap

"She read it again, dully, as though every selfish word had not
already stamped itself on her brain and heart"—*Page 204*

of her blue serge skirt — brushed, and brushed, and brushed, with a mechanical, pathetic little gesture that showed how completely absent her mind was from the room in which she sat. Then her hand fell idle, and she became very still, a crumpled, tragic, hopeless look rounding the shoulders that were wont to hold themselves so erect and confident.

A tentative knock at the door. The figure on the bed did not stir. Another knock, louder this time. Emma McChesney sat up with a start. She shivered as she became conscious of the icy December air pouring into the little room. She rose, walked to the window, closed it with a bang, and opened the door in time to intercept the third knock.

A waiter proffered her a long card. " Dinner, Madame? "

" Oh! " She shook her head. " Sorry. I've changed my mind. I — I shan't want any dinner."

She shut the door again and stood with her back against it, eying the bed. In her mind's eye she had already thrown herself upon it, buried her face in the nest of pillows, and given vent to the flood of tears that was beating at her throat. She took a quick step toward the bed, stopped, turned abruptly, and walked toward the mirror.

"Emma McChesney," she said aloud to the woman in the glass, "buck up, old girl! Bad luck comes in bunches of threes. It's like breaking the first cup in a new Haviland set. You can always count on smashing two more. This is your third. So pick up the pieces and throw 'em in the ash-can."

Then she fastened her collar, buttoned her shoe, pulled down her shirtwaist all around, smeared her face with cold cream, wiped it with a towel, smoothed her hair, donned her hat. The next instant the little room was dark, and Emma McChesney was marching down the long, red-carpeted hallway to the elevator, her head high, her face set.

Down-stairs in the lobby — "How about my trunks?" she inquired of a porter.

That blue-shirted individual rubbed a hard brown hand over his cheek worriedly.

"They ain't come."

"Ain't come!"— surprise disregarded grammar.

"Nope. No signs of 'em. I'll tell you

what: I think prob'ly they was overlooked in the rush, the train being late from Dayton when you started. Likely they'll be in on the ten-thirteen. I'll send 'em up the minute they get in."

" I wish you would. I've got to get my stuff out early. I can't keep customers waiting for me. Late, as it is."

She approached the clerk once more. " Anything at the theaters? "

" Well, nothing much, Mrs. McChesney. Christmas coming on kind of puts a crimp in the show business. Nice little bill on at the Majestic, if you like vaudeville."

" Crazy about it. Always get so excited watching to see if the next act is going to be as rotten as the last one. It always is."

From eight-fifteen until ten-thirty Mrs. Mc-Chesney sat absolutely expressionless while a shrill blonde lady and a nasal dark gentleman went through what the program ironically called a " comedy sketch," followed by a chummy person who came out in evening dress to sing a sentimental ditty, shed the evening dress to reappear in an ankle-length fluffy pink affair; shucked the fluffy pink affair for a child's pina-

[209]

fore, sash, and bare knees; discarded the kiddie frock, disclosing a bathing-suit; left the bathing-suit behind the wings in favor of satin knee-breeches and tight jacket — and very discreetly stopped there, probably for no reason except to give way to the next act, consisting of two miraculously thin young men in lavender dress suits and white silk hats, who sang and clogged in unison, like two things hung on a single wire.

The night air was grateful to her hot forehead as she walked from the theater to the hotel.

" Trunks in? " to the porter.

" No sign of 'em, lady. They didn't come in on the ten. Think they'd better wire back to Dayton."

But the next morning Mrs. McChesney was in the depot baggage-room when Dayton wired back:

" *Trunks not here. Try Columbus, Nebraska.*"

" Crash! " said Emma McChesney to the surprised baggage-master. " There goes my Haviland vegetable-dish."

" Were you selling china? " he inquired.

" No, I wasn't," replied Emma McChesney

viciously. " And if you don't let me stand here and give my frank, unbiased opinion of this road, its president, board of directors, stockholders, baggage-men, Pullman porters, and other things thereto appertaining, I'll probably have hysterics."

" Give it," said the baggage-master. " You'll feel better. And we're used to it."

She gave it. When she had finished:

" Did you say you was selling goods on the road? Say, that's a hell of a job for a woman! Excuse me, lady. I didn't mean —"

" I think perhaps you're right," said Emma McChesney slowly. " It is just that."

" Well, anyway, we'll do our best to trace it. Guess you're in for a wait."

Emma McChesney waited. She made the rounds of her customers, and waited. She wired her firm, and waited. She wrote Jock to run along and enjoy himself, and waited. She cut and fitted a shirt-waist, took her hat apart and retrimmed it, made the rounds of her impatient customers again, threatened to sue the road, visited the baggage-room daily — and waited.

Four weary, nerve-racking days passed. It

was late afternoon of the fourth day when Mrs.
McChesney entered the elevator to go to her
room. She had come from another fruitless
visit to the baggage-room. She sank into a
leather-cushioned seat in a corner of the lift.
Two men entered briskly, followed by a bell-
boy. Mrs. McChesney did not look up.

"Well, I'll be dinged!" boomed a throaty
voice. "Mrs. McChesney, by the Great Horn
Spoon! H'are you? Talking about you this
minute to my friend here."

Emma McChesney, with the knowledge of
her lost sample-trunks striking her afresh,
looked up and smiled bravely into the plump
pink face of Fat Ed Meyers, traveling representative for her firm's bitterest rival, the Strauss
Sans-silk Skirt Company.

"Talking about me, Mr. Meyers? Sufficient grounds for libel, right there."

The little sallow, dark man just at Meyers'
elbow was gazing at her unguardedly. She
felt that he had appraised her from hat to heels.
Ed Meyers placed a plump hand on the little
man's shoulder.

"Abe, you tell the lady what I was saying.
This is Mr. Abel Fromkin, maker of the From-

kin Form-Fit Skirt. Abe, this is the wonderful Mrs. McChesney."

"Sorry I can't wait to hear what you've said of me. This is my floor." Mrs. McChesney was already leaving the elevator.

"Here! Wait a minute!" Fat Ed Meyers was out and standing beside her, his movements unbelievably nimble. "Will you have dinner with us, Mrs. McChesney?"

"Thanks. Not to-night."

Meyers turned to the waiting elevator. "Fromkin, you go on up with the boy; I'll talk to the lady a minute."

A little displeased frown appeared on Emma McChesney's face.

"You'll have to excuse me, **Mr. Meyers**, I —"

"Heigh-ho for that haughty stuff, Mrs. McChesney," grinned Ed Meyers. "Don't turn up your nose at that little Kike friend of mine till you've heard what I have to say. Now just let me talk a minute. Fromkin's heard all about you. He's got a proposition to make. And it isn't one to sniff at."

He lowered his voice mysteriously in the silence of the dim hotel corridor.

[213]

CATCHING UP WITH CHRISTMAS

" Fromkin started in a little one-room hole-in-the-wall over on the East Side. Lived on a herring and a hunk of rye bread. Wife used to help him sew. That was seven years ago. In three years, or less, she'll have the regulation uniform — full length seal coat, bunch of paradise, five-drop diamond La Valliere set in platinum, electric brougham. Abe has got a business head, take it from me. But he's wise enough to know that business isn't the rough-and-tumble game it used to be. He realizes that he'll do for the workrooms, but not for the front shop. He knows that if he wants to keep on growing he's got to have what they call a steerer. Somebody smooth, and polished, and politic, and what the highbrows call suave. Do you pronounce that with a long *a*, or two dots over? Anyway, you get me. You're all those things and considerable few besides. He's wise to the fact that a business man's got to have poise these days, and balance. And when it comes to poise and balance, Mrs. McChesney, you make a Fairbanks scale look like a raft at sea."

" While I don't want to seem to hurry you," drawled Mrs. McChesney, " might I suggest that you shorten the overture and begin on the first act?"

"Well, you know how I feel about your business genius."

"Yes, I know," enigmatically.

Ed Meyers grinned. "Can't forget those two little business misunderstandings we had, can you?"

"Business understandings," corrected Emma McChesney.

"Call 'em anything your little heart dictates, but listen. Fromkin knows all about you. Knows you've got a million friends in the trade, that you know skirts from the belt to the hem. I don't know just what his proposition is, but I'll bet he'll give you half interest in the livest, come-upest little skirt factory in the country, just for a few thousands capital, maybe, and your business head at the executive end. Now just let that sink in before you speak."

"And why," inquired Emma McChesney, "don't you grab this matchless business opportunity yourself?"

"Because, fair lady, Fromkin wouldn't let me get in with a crowbar. He'll never be able to pronounce his t's right, and when he's dressed up he looks like a 'bus-boy at Mouquin's, but he can see a bluff farther than I can throw one — and that's somewhere beyond the horizon, as you'll admit. Talk it over with us after dinner then?"

Emma McChesney was regarding the plump, pink, eager face before her with keen, level, searching eyes.

"Yes," she said slowly, "I will."

"Café? We'll have a bottle —"

"No."

"Oh! Er — parlor?"

Mrs. McChesney smiled. "I won't ask you to make yourself that miserable. You can't smoke in the parlor. We'll find a quiet corner in the writing-room, where you men can light up. I don't want to take advantage of you."

Down in the writing-room at eight they formed a strange little group. Ed Meyers, flushed and eager, his pink face glowing like a peony, talking, arguing, smoking, reasoning, coaxing, with the spur of a fat commission to urge him on; Abel Fromkin, with his peculiarly pallid skin made paler in contrast to the pur-plish-black line where the razor had passed, showing no hint of excitement except in the restless little black eyes and in the work-scarred hands that rolled cigarette after cigarette, each glowing for one brief instant, only to die down to a blackened ash the next; Emma McChesney, half fascinated, half distrustful, listening in spite of herself, and trying to still a small inner voice — a voice that had never advised her ill.

" You know the ups and downs to this game," Ed Meyers was saying. " When I met you there in the elevator you looked like you'd lost your last customer. You get pretty disgusted with it all, at times, like the rest of us."

" At that minute," replied Emma McChesney, " I was so disgusted that if some one had called me up on the 'phone and said, ' Hullo, Mrs. McChesney! Will you marry me? ' I'd have said: ' Yes. Who is this? ' "

" There! That's just it. I don't want to be impolite, or anything like that, Mrs. McChesney, but you're no kid. Not that you look your age — not by ten years! But I happen to know you're teetering somewhere between thirty-six and the next top. Ain't that right? "

CATCHING UP WITH CHRISTMAS

"Is that a argument to put to a lady?" remonstrated Abel Fromkin.

Fat Ed Meyers waved the interruption away with a gesture of his strangely slim hands.

"This ain't an argument. It's facts. Another ten years on the road, and where'll you be? In the discard. A man of forty-six can keep step with the youngsters, even if it does make him puff a bit. But a woman of forty-six — the road isn't the place for her. She's tired. Tired in the morning; tired at night. She wants her kimono and her afternoon snooze. You've seen some of those old girls on the road. They've come down step by step until you spot 'em, bleached hair, crow's-feet around the eyes, mussy shirt-waist, yellow and red complexion, demonstrating green and lavender gelatine messes in the grocery of some department store. I don't say that a brainy corker of a saleswoman like you would come down like that. But you've got to consider sickness and a lot of other things. Those six weeks last summer with the fever at Glen Rock put a crimp in you, didn't it? You've never been yourself since then. Haven't had a decent chance to rest up."

"No," said Emma McChesney wearily.

" 'Not that you look your age—not by ten years!' "—*Page 217*

CATCHING UP WITH CHRISTMAS

" Furthermore, now that old T. A.'s cashed in, how do you know what young Buck's going to do? He don't know shucks about the skirt business. They've got to take in a third party to keep it a close corporation. It was all between old Buck, Buck junior, and old lady Buck. How can you tell whether the new member will want a woman on the road, or not?"

A little steely light hardened the blue of Mrs. McChesney's eyes.

"We'll leave the firm of T. A. Buck out of this discussion, please."

"Oh, very well!" Ed Meyers was unabashed. "Let's talk about Fromkin. He don't object, do you, Abe? It's just like this. He needs your smart head. You need his money. It'll mean a sure thing for you — a share in a growing and substantial business. When you get your road men trained it'll mean that you won't need to go out on the road yourself, except for a little missionary trip now and then, maybe. No more infernal early trains, no more bum hotel grub, no more stuffy, hot hotel rooms, no more haughty lady buyers — gosh, I wish I had the chance!"

Emma McChesney sat very still. Two scarlet spots glowed in her cheeks. "No one appreciates your gift of oratory more than I do, Mr. Meyers. Your flow of language, coupled with your peculiar persuasive powers, make a combination a statue couldn't resist. But I think it would sort of rest me if Mr. Fromkin were to say a word, seeing that it's really his funeral."

Abel Fromkin started nervously, and put his dead cigarette to his lips. "I ain't much of a talker," he said, almost sheepishly. "Meyers, he's got it down fine. I tell you what. I'll be in New York the twenty-first. We can go over the books and papers and the whole business. And I like you should know my wife. And I got a little girl — Would you believe it, that child ain't more as a year old, and says Papa and Mama like a actress!"

"Sure," put in Ed Meyers, disregarding the more intimate family details. "You two get together and fix things up in shape; then you can sign up and have it off your mind so you can enjoy the festive Christmas season."

Emma McChesney had been gazing out of the window to where the street-lamps were reflected in the ice-covered pavements.   Now she spoke, still staring out upon the wintry street.

"Christmas isn't a season.   It's a feeling. And I haven't got it."

"Oh, come now, Mrs. McChesney!" objected Ed Meyers.

With a sudden, quick movement Emma McChesney turned from the window to the little dark man who was watching her so intently. She faced him squarely, as though utterly disregarding Ed Meyers' flattery and banter and cajolery.   The little man before her seemed to recognize the earnestness of the moment.   He leaned forward a bit attentively.

"If what has been said is true," she began, "this ought to be a good thing for me.   If I go into it, I'll go in heart, soul, brain, and pocket-book.   I do know the skirt business from thread to tape and back again.   I've managed to save a few thousand dollars.   Only a woman could understand how I've done it.   I've scrimped on little things.   I've denied myself necessities.   I've worn silk blouses instead of linen ones to save laundry-bills and taken a street-car or 'bus to save a quarter or fifty cents.

I've always tried to look well dressed and immaculate —"

" You! " exclaimed Ed Meyers. " Why,
say, you're what I call a swell dresser. Nothing flashy, understand, or loud, but the quiet,.
good stuff that spells ready money."

" M-m-m — yes. But it wasn't always so
ready. Anyway, I always managed somehow.
The boy's at college. Sometimes I wonder —
well, that's another story. I've saved, and con-
trived, and planned ahead for a rainy day.
There have been two or three times when I
thought it had come. Sprinkled pretty heavily,
once or twice. But I've just turned up my coat-
collar, tucked my hat under my skirt, and scooted
for a tree. And each time it has turned out to
be just a summer shower, with the sun coming
out bright and warm."

Her frank, clear, honest, blue eyes were
plumbing the depths of the black ones. " Those
few thousand dollars that you hold so lightly
will mean everything to me. They've been my
cyclone-cellar. If —"

Through the writing-room sounded a high-
pitched, monotonous voice with a note of in-
quiry in it.

CATCHING UP WITH CHRISTMAS

"Mrs. McChesney! Mr. Fraser! Mr. Ludwig! Please! Mrs. McChesney! Mr. Fraser! Mr. Lud—"

"Here, boy!" Mrs. McChesney took the little yellow envelope from the salver that the boy held out to her. Her quick glance rested on the written words. She rose, her face colorless.

"Not bad news?" The two men spoke simultaneously.

"I don't know," said Emma McChesney. "What would you say?"

She handed the slip of paper to Fat Ed Meyers. He read it in silence. Then once more, aloud:

"'Take first train back to New York. Spalding will finish your trip.'"

"Why — say — " began Meyers.

"Well?"

"Why — say — this — this looks as if you were fired!"

"Does, doesn't it?" She smiled.

"Then our little agreement goes?" The two men were on their feet, eager, alert. "That means you'll take Fromkin's offer?"

" It means that our little agreement is off.
I'm sorry to disappoint you. I want to thank
you both for your trouble. I must have been
crazy to listen to you for a minute. I wouldn't
have if I'd been myself."

" But that telegram —"

" It's signed, ' T. A. Buck.' I'll take a
chance."

The two men stared after her, disappointment and bewilderment chasing across each face.

" Well, I thought I knew women, but —"
began Ed Meyers fluently.

Passing the desk, Mrs. McChesney heard
her name. She glanced toward the clerk. He
was just hanging up the telephone-receiver.
" Baggage-room says the depot just notified 'em
your trunks were traced to Columbia City.
They're on their way here now."

" Columbia City! " repeated Emma Mc-
Chesney. " Do you know, I believe I've
learned to hate the name of the discoverer of
this fair land."

Up in her room she opened the crumpled
telegram again, and regarded it thoughtfully
before she began to pack her bag.

The thoughtful look was still there when she

entered the big bright office of the T. A. Buck
Featherloom Petticoat Company. And with it
was another expression that resembled contri-
tion.

"Mr. Buck's waiting for you," a stenographer told her.

Mrs. McChesney opened the door of the office marked "Private."

Two men rose. One she recognized as the
firm's lawyer. The other, who came swiftly
toward her, was T. A. Buck — no longer junior.
There was a new look about him — a look of
responsibility, of efficiency, of clear-headed
knowledge.

The two clasped hands — a firm, sincere,
understanding grip.

Buck spoke first. "It's good to see you.
We were talking of you as you came in. You
know Mr. Beggs, of course. He has some
things to tell you — and so have I. His will
be business things, mine will be personal. I got
there before father passed away — thank God!
But he couldn't speak. He'd anticipated that
with his clear-headedness, and he'd written what
he wanted to say. A great deal of it was about
you. I want you to read that letter later."

" I shall consider it a privilege," said Emma McChesney.

Mr. Beggs waved her toward a chair. She took it in silence. She heard him in silence, his sonorous voice beating upon her brain.

" There are a great many papers and much business detail, but that will be attended to later," began Beggs ponderously. " You are to be congratulated on the position of esteem and trust which you held in the mind of your late employer. By the terms of his will — I'll put it briefly, for the moment — you are offered the secretaryship of the firm of T. A. Buck, Incorporated. Also you are bequeathed thirty shares in the firm. Of course, the company will have to be reorganized. The late Mr. Buck had great trust in your capabilities."

Emma McChesney rose to her feet, her breath coming quickly. She turned to T. A. Buck. " I want you to know — I want you to know — that just before your telegram came I was half tempted to leave the firm. To —"

" Can't blame you," smiled T. A. Buck. " You've had a rotten six months of it, beginning with that illness and ending with those in-

"'Christmas isn't a season . . ., it's a feeling; and, thank God, I've got it!'"—*Page 229*

fernal trunks. The road's no place for a woman."

"Nonsense!" flashed Emma McChesney. "I've loved it. I've gloried in it. And I've earned my living by it. Giving it up — don't now think me ungrateful — won't be so easy, I can tell you."

T. A. Buck nodded understandingly. "I know. Father knew too. And I don't want you to let his going from us make any difference in this holiday season. I want you to enjoy it and be happy."

A shade crossed Emma McChesney's face. It was there when the door opened and a boy entered with a telegram. He handed it to Mrs. McChesney. It held ten crisp words:

Changed my darn fool mind. Me for home and mother.

Emma McChesney looked up, her face radiant.

"Christmas isn't a season, Mr. Buck. It's a feeling; and, thank God, I've got it!"

IX

KNEE-DEEP IN KNICKERS

WHEN the column of figures under the heading known as " Profits," and the column of figures under the heading known as " Loss " are so unevenly balanced that the wrong side of the ledger sags, then to the listening stockholders there comes the painful thought that at the next regular meeting it is perilously possible that the reading may come under the heads of Assets and Liabilities.

There had been a meeting in the offices of the T. A. Buck Featherloom Petticoat Company, New York. The quarterly report had had a startlingly lop-sided sound. After it was over Mrs. Emma McChesney, secretary of the company, followed T. A. Buck, its president, into the big, bright show-room. T. A. Buck's hands were thrust deep into his pockets. His teeth worried a cigar, savagely. Care, that clawing, mouthing hag, perched on his brow, tore at his heart.

He turned to face Emma McChesney.

" Well," he said, bitterly, " it hasn't taken us long, has it? Father's been dead a little over a year. In that time we've just about run this great concern, the pride of his life, into the ground."

Mrs. Emma McChesney, calm, cool, unruffled, scrutinized the harassed man before her for a long minute.

" What rotten football material you would have made, wouldn't you? " she observed.

" Oh, I don't know," answered T. A. Buck, through his teeth. " I can stand as stiff a scrimmage as the next one. But this isn't a game. You take things too lightly. You're a woman. I don't think you know what this means."

Emma McChesney's lips opened as do those of one whose tongue's end holds a quick and stinging retort. Then they closed again. She walked over to the big window that faced the street. When she had stood there a moment, silent, she swung around and came back to where T. A. Buck stood, still wrapped in gloom.

"Maybe I don't take myself seriously. I'd have been dead ten years ago if I had. But I do take my job seriously. Don't forget that for a minute. You talk the way a man always talks when his pride is hurt."

"Pride! It isn't that."

"Oh, yes, it is. I didn't sell T. A. Buck's Featherloom Petticoats on the road for almost ten years without learning a little something about men and business. When your father died, and I learned that he had shown his appreciation of my work and loyalty by making me secretary of this great company, I didn't think of it as a legacy — a stroke of good fortune."

"No?"

"No. To me it was a sacred trust — something to be guarded, nursed, cherished. And now you say we've run this concern into the ground. Do you honestly think that?"

T. A. shrugged impotent shoulders. "Figures don't lie." He plunged into another fathom of gloom. "Another year like this and we're done for."

Emma McChesney came over and put one firm hand on T. A. Buck's drooping shoulder.

KNEE-DEEP IN KNICKERS

It was a strange little act for a woman — the sort of thing a man does when he would hearten another man.

"Wake up!" she said, lightly. "Wake up, and listen to the birdies sing. There isn't going to be another year like this. Not if the planning, and scheming, and brain-racking that I've been doing for the last two or three months mean anything."

T. A. Buck seated himself as one who is weary, body and mind.

"Got another new one?"

Emma McChesney regarded him a moment thoughtfully. Then she stepped to the tall show-case, pushed back the sliding glass door, and pointed to the rows of brilliant-hued petticoats that hung close-packed within.

"Look at 'em!" she commanded, disgust in her voice. "Look at 'em!"

T. A. Buck raised heavy, lack-luster eyes and looked. What he saw did not seem to interest him. Emma McChesney drew from the rack a skirt of king's blue satin messaline and held it at arm's length.

"And they call that thing a petticoat! Why, fifteen years ago the material in this skirt

[233]

wouldn't have made even a fair-sized sleeve."

T. A. Buck regarded the petticoat moodily. "I don't see how they get around in the darned things. I honestly don't see how they wear 'em."

"That's just it. They don't wear 'em. There you have the root of the whole trouble."

"Oh, nonsense!" disputed T. A. "They certainly wear something — some sort of an —"

"I tell you they don't. Here. Listen. Three years ago our taffeta skirts ran from thirty-six to thirty-eight yards to the dozen. We paid from ninety cents to one dollar five a yard. Now our skirts run from twenty-five to twenty-eight yards to the dozen. The silk costs us from fifty to sixty cents a yard. Silk skirts used to be a luxury. Now they're not even a necessity."

"Well, what's the answer? I've been pondering some petticoat problems myself. I know we've got to sell three skirts to-day to make the profit that we used to make on one three years ago."

Emma McChesney had the brave-heartedness to laugh. "This skirt business reminds me of a game we used to play when I was a kid.

KNEE-DEEP IN KNICKERS

We called it Going to Jerusalem, I think. Anyway, I know each child sat in a chair except the one who was It. At a signal everybody had to get up and change chairs. There was a wild scramble, in which the one who was It took part. When the hurly-burly was over some child was always chairless, of course. He had to be It. That's the skirt business to-day. There aren't enough chairs to go round, and in the scramble somebody's got to be left out. And let me tell you, here and now, that the firm of T. A. Buck, Featherloom Petticoats, is not going to be It."

T. A. rose as wearily as he had sat down. Even the most optimistic of watchers could have discerned no gleam of enthusiasm on his face.

" I thought," he said listlessly, " that you and I had tried every possible scheme to stimulate the skirt trade."

" Every possible one, yes," agreed Mrs. Mc-Chesney, sweetly. " And now it's time to try the impossible. The possibilities haven't worked. My land! I could write a book on the Decline and Fall of the Petticoat, beginning with the billowy white muslin variety, and working up to the present slinky messaline affair. When I think of those dear dead days of the glorious — er — past, when the hired girl used to complain and threaten to leave because every woman in the family had at least three ruffled, embroidery-flounced white muslin petticoats on the line on Mondays —"

The lines about T. A. Buck's mouth relaxed into a grim smile.

" Remember that feature you got them to run in the *Sunday Sphere?* The one headed ' Are Skirts Growing Fuller, and Where? ' "

" Do I remember it ! " wailed Emma Mc- Chesney. " And can I ever forget the money we put into that fringed model we called the Carmencita ! We made it up so it could retail for a dollar ninety-five, and I could have sworn that the women would maim each other to get to it. But it didn't go. They won't even wear fringe around their ankles."

T. A.'s grim smile stretched into a reminiscent grin. " But nothing in our whole hopeless campaign could touch your Municipal Purity League agitation for the abolition of the form-hugging skirt. You talked public morals until you had A. Comstock and Lucy Page Gaston looking like Parisian Apaches."

A little laugh rippled up to Emma McChesney's lips, only to die away to a sigh. She shook her head in sorrowful remembrance.

"Yes. But what good did it do? The newspapers and magazines did take it up, but what happened? The dressmakers and tailors, who are charging more than ever for their work, and putting in half as much material, got together and knocked my plans into a cocked hat. In answer to those snap-shots showing what took place every time a woman climbed a car step, they came back with pictures of the styles of '61, proving that the street-car effect is nothing to what happened to a belle of '61 if she chanced to sit down or get up too suddenly in the hoop-skirt days."

They were both laughing now, like a couple of children. "And, oh, say!" gasped Emma, " remember Moe Selig, of the Fine-Form Skirt Company, trying to get the doctors to state that hobble skirts were making women knock-kneed! Oh, mercy!"

But their laugh ended in a little rueful silence. It was no laughing matter, this situation. T. A. Buck shrugged his shoulders, and began a restless pacing up and down. "Yep. There you are. Meanwhile —"

" Meanwhile, women are still wearing 'em tight, and going petticoatless."

Suddenly T. A. stopped short in his pacing and fastened his surprised and interested gaze on the skirt of the trim and correct little business frock that sat so well upon Emma McChesney's pretty figure.

" Why, look at that! " he exclaimed, and pointed with one eager finger.

" Mercy! " screamed Emma McChesney. " What is it? Quick! A mouse? "

T. A. Buck shook his head, impatiently. " Mouse! Lord, no! Plaits! "

" Plaits! "

She looked down, bewildered.

" Yes. In your skirt. Three plaits at the front-left, and three in the back. That's new, isn't it? If outer skirts are being made fuller, then it follows —"

" It ought to follow," interrupted Emma McChesney, " but it doesn't. It lags way behind. These plaits are stitched down. See? That's the fiendishness of it. And the petticoat underneath — if there is one — must be just as smooth, and unwrinkled, and scant as ever. Don't let 'em fool you."

Buck spread his palms with a little gesture of utter futility.

"I'm through. Out with your scheme. We're ready for it. It's our last card, whatever it is."

There was visible on Emma McChesney's face that little tightening of the muscles, that narrowing of the eyelids which betokens intense earnestness; the gathering of all the forces before taking a momentous step. Then, as quickly, her face cleared. She shook her head with a little air of sudden decision.

"Not now. Just because it's our last card I want to be sure that I'm playing it well. I'll be ready for you to-morrow morning in my office. Come prepared for the jolt of your young life."

For the first time since the beginning of the conversation a glow of new courage and hope lighted up T. A. Buck's good-looking features. His fine eyes rested admiringly upon Emma McChesney standing there by the great show-case. She seemed to radiate energy, alertness, confidence.

"When you begin to talk like that," he said, "I always feel as though I could take hold in a way to make those famous jobs that Hercules tackled look like little Willie's chores after school."

"Fine!" beamed Emma McChesney. "Just store that up, will you? And don't let it filter out at your finger-tips when I begin to talk to-morrow."

"We'll have lunch together, eh? And talk it over then sociably."

Mrs. McChesney closed the glass door of the case with a bang.

"No, thanks. My office at 9:30."

T. A. Buck followed her to the door. "But why not lunch? You never will take lunch with me. Ever so much more comfortable to talk things over that way —"

"When I talk business," said Emma McChesney, pausing at the threshold, "I want to be surrounded by a business atmosphere. I want the scene all set — one practical desk, two practical chairs, one telephone, one letter-basket, one self-filling fountain-pen, et cetera. And when I lunch I want to lunch, with nothing weightier on my mind than the question as to whether I'll have chicken livers sauté or creamed sweetbreads with mushrooms."

"That's no reason," grumbled T. A. "That's an excuse."

"It will have to do, though," replied Mrs. McChesney abruptly, and passed out as he held the door open for her. He was still standing in the doorway after her trim, erect figure had disappeared into the little office across the hall.

The little scarlet leather clock on Emma McChesney's desk pointed to 9:29 A.M. when there entered her office an immaculately garbed, miraculously shaven, healthily rosy youngish-middle-aged man who looked ten years younger than the harassed, frowning T. A. Buck with whom she had almost quarreled the evening be-fore. Mrs. McChesney was busily dictating to a sleek little stenographer. The sleek little stenographer glanced up at T. A. Buck's entrance. The glance, being a feminine one, embraced all of T. A.'s good points and approved them from the tips of his modish boots to the crown of his slightly bald head, and including the creamy-white flower that reposed in his buttonhole.

"'Morning!" said Emma McChesney, looking up briefly. "Be with you in a minute. . . . and in reply would say we regret that you have had trouble with No. 339. It is impossible to avoid pulling at the seams in the lower-grade silk skirts when they are made up in the present scant style. Our Mr. Spalding warned you of this at the time of your purchase. We will not under any circumstances consent to receive the goods if they are sent back on our hands. Yours sincerely. That'll be all, Miss Casey."

She swung around to face her visitor as the door closed. If T. A. Buck looked ten years younger than he had the afternoon before, Emma McChesney undoubtedly looked five years older. There were little, worried, sagging lines about her eyes and mouth.

T. A. Buck's eyes had followed the sheaf of signed correspondence, and the well-filled pad of more recent dictation which the sleek little stenographer had carried away with her.

" Good Lord! It looks as though you had stayed down here all night."

Emma McChesney smiled a little wearily. " Not quite that. But I was here this morning in time to greet the night watchman. Wanted to get my mail out of the way." Her eyes searched T. A. Buck's serene face. Then she leaned forward, earnestly.

"Haven't you seen the morning paper?"

"Just a mere glance at 'em. Picked up Burrows on the way down, and we got to talking. Why?"

"The Rasmussen-Welsh Skirt Company has failed. Liabilities three hundred thousand. Assets one hundred thousand."

"Failed! Good God!" All the rosy color, all the brisk morning freshness had vanished from his face. "Failed! Why, girl, I thought that concern was as solid as Gibraltar." He passed a worried hand over his head. "That knocks the wind out of my sails."

"Don't let it. Just say that it fills them with a new breeze. I'm all the more sure that the time is ripe for my plan."

T. A. Buck took from a vest pocket a scrap of paper and a fountain pen, slid down in his chair, crossed his legs, and began to scrawl meaningless twists and curlycues, as was his wont when worried or deeply interested.

"Are you as sure of this scheme of yours as you were yesterday?"

" Sure," replied Emma McChesney, briskly. " Sartin-sure."

" Then fire away."

Mrs. McChesney leaned forward, breathing a trifle fast. Her eyes were fastened on her listener.

" Here's the plan. We'll make Feather-loom Petticoats because there still are some women who have kept their senses. But we'll make them as a side line. The thing that has got to keep us afloat until full skirts come in again will be a full and complete line of women's satin messaline knickerbockers made up to match any suit or gown, and a full line of pajamas for women and girls. Get the idea? Scant, smart, trim little taupe-gray messaline knickers for a taupe gray suit, blue messaline for blue suits, brown messaline for brown —"

T. A. Buck stared, open-mouthed, the paper on which he had been scrawling fluttering unnoticed to the floor.

" Look here! " he interrupted. " Is this supposed to be humorous? "

" And," went on Emma McChesney, calmly, " in our full and complete, not to say nifty line of women's pajamas — pink pajamas, blue pajamas, violet pajamas, yellow pajamas, white silk —"

T. A. Buck stood up. " I want to say," he began, " that if you are jesting, I think this is a mighty poor time to joke. And if you are serious I can only deduce from it that this year of business worry and responsibility has been too much for you. I'm sure that if you were —"

" That's all right," interrupted Emma Mc-Chesney. " Don't apologize. I purposely broke it to you this way, when I might have approached it gently. You've done just what I knew you'd do, so it's all right. After you've thought it over, and sort of got chummy with the idea, you'll be just as keen on it as I am."

" Never! "

" Oh, yes, you will. It's the knickerbocker end of it that scares you. Nothing new or startling about pajamas, except that more and more women are wearing 'em, and that no girl would dream of going away to school without her six sets of pajamas. Why, a girl in a regulation nightie at one of their midnight spreads would be ostracized. Of course I've thought up a couple of new kinks in 'em — new ways of

[245]

cutting and all that, and there's one model — a washable crêpe, for traveling, that doesn't need to be pressed — but I'll talk about that later."

T. A. Buck was trying to put in a word of objection, but she would have none of it. But at Emma McChesney's next words his indignation would brook no barriers.

" Now," she went on, " the feature of the knickerbockers will be this: They've got to be ready for the boys' spring trip, and in all the larger cities, especially in the hustling Middle-Western towns, and along the coast, too, I'm planning to have the knickerbockers introduced at private and exclusive exhibitions, and worn by — get this, please — worn by living models. One big store in each town, see? Half a dozen good-looking girls —"

" Never! " shouted T. A. Buck, white and shaking. " Never! This firm has always had a name for dignity, solidness, conservatism —"

" Then it's just about time it lost that reputation. It's all very well to hang on to your dignity when you're on solid ground, but when you feel things slipping from under you the thing to do is to grab on to anything that'll keep you on your feet for a while at least. I tell you the women will go wild over this knickerbocker idea. They've been waiting for it."

"It's a wild-cat scheme," disputed Buck hotly. "It's a drowning man's straw, and just about as helpful. I'm a reasonable man —"

"All unreasonable men say that," smiled Emma McChesney.

"— I'm a reasonable man, I say. And heaven knows I have the interest of this firm at heart. But this is going too far. If we're going to smash we'll go decently, and with our name untarnished. Pajamas are bad enough. But when it comes to the firm of T. A. Buck being represented by — by — living model hussies stalking about in satin tights like chorus girls, why —"

In Emma McChesney's alert, electric mind there leapt about a dozen plans for winning this man over. For win him she would, in the end. It was merely a question of method. She chose the simplest. There was a set look about her jaw. Her eyes flashed. Two spots of carmine glowed in her cheeks.

"I expected just this," she said. "And I prepared for it." She crossed swiftly to her desk, opened a drawer, and took out a flat package. " I expected opposition. That's why I had these samples made up to show you. I designed them myself, and tore up fifty patterns before I struck one that suited me. Here are the pajamas."

She lifted out a dainty, shell-pink garment, and shook it out before the half-interested, half-unwilling eyes of T. A. Buck.

" This is the jacket. Buttons on the left; see? Instead of the right, as it would in a man's garment. Semi-sailor collar, with knotted soft silk scarf. Oh, it's just a little kink, but they'll love it. They're actually becoming. I've tried 'em. Notice the frogs and cord. Pretty neat, yes? Slight flare at the hips. Makes 'em set and hang right. Perfectly straight, like a man's coat."

T. A. Buck eyed the garments with a grudging admiration.

" Oh, that part of it don't sound so unreasonable, although I don't believe there is much of a demand for that kind of thing. But the other — the — the knickerbocker things — that's not even practical. It will make an ugly garment, and the women who would fall for a fad like that wouldn't be of the sort to wear an ugly piece of lingerie. It isn't to be thought of seriously —"

Emma McChesney stepped to the door of the tiny wash-room off her office and threw it open.

" Miss La Noyes! We're ready for you."

And there emerged from the inner room a trim, lithe, almost boyishly slim figure attired in a bewitchingly skittish-looking garment consisting of knickerbockers and snug brassière of king's blue satin messaline. Dainty black silk stockings and tiny buckled slippers set off the whole effect.

" Miss La Noyes," said Emma McChesney, almost solemnly, " this is Mr. T. A. Buck, president of the firm. Miss La Noyes, of the ' Gay Social Whirl ' company."

Miss La Noyes bowed slightly and rested one white hand at her side in an attitude of nonchalant ease.

" Pleased, I'm shaw! " she said, in a clear, high voice.

And, " Charmed," replied T. A. Buck, his years and breeding standing him in good stead now.

Emma McChesney laid a kindly hand on the

girl's shoulder. "Turn slowly, please. Observe the absence of unnecessary fulness about the hips, or at the knees. No wrinkles to show there. No man will ever appreciate the fine points of this little garment, but the women! — To the left, Miss La Noyes. You'll see it fastens snug and trim with a tiny clasp just below the knees. This garment has the added attraction of being fastened to the upper garment, a tight satin brassière. The single, unattached garment is just as satisfactory, however. Women are wearing plush this year. Not only for the street, but for evening dresses. I rather think they'll fancy a snappy little pair of yellow satin knickers under a gown of the new orange plush. Or a taupe pair, under a gray street suit. Or a natty little pair of black satin, finished and piped in white satin, to be worn with a black and white shopping costume. Why, I haven't worn a petticoat since I —"

"Do you mean to tell me," burst from the long-pent T. A. Buck, "that you wear 'em too?"

"Crazy about 'em. Miss La Noyes, will you just slip on your street skirt, please?"

She waited in silence until the demure Miss

" 'No man will ever appreciate the fine points of this little garment, but the women—!' "—*Page 250*

La Noyes reappeared. A narrow, straight-hanging, wrinkleless cloth skirt covered the much discussed under-garment. " Turn slowly, please. Thanks. You see, Mr. Buck? Not a wrinkle. No bunchiness. No lumps. No crawling up about the knees. Nothing but ease, and comfort, and trim good looks."

T. A. Buck passed his hand over his head in a dazed, helpless gesture. There was something pathetic in his utter bewilderment and helplessness in contrast with Emma McChesney's breezy self-confidence, and the show-girl's cool poise and unconcern.

" Wait a minute," he murmured, almost pleadingly. " Let me ask a couple of questions, will you? "

" Questions? A hundred. That proves you're interested."

" Well, then, let me ask this young lady the first one. Miss — er — La Noyes, do you honestly and truly like this garment? Would you buy one if you saw it in a shop window? "

Miss La Noyes' answer came trippingly and without hesitation. She did not even have to feel of her back hair first.

" Say, I'd go without my lunch for a week to

get it. Mrs. McChesney says I can have this pair. I can't wait till our prima donna sees 'em. She'll hate me till she's got a dozen like 'em."

"Next!" urged Mrs. McChesney, pleasantly.

But T. A. Buck shook his head. "That's all. Only —"

Emma McChesney patted Miss La Noyes lightly on the shoulder, and smiled dazzlingly upon her. "Run along, little girl. You've done beautifully. And many thanks."

Miss La Noyes, appearing in another moment dressed for the street, stopped at the door to bestow a frankly admiring smile upon the abstracted president of the company, and a grateful one upon its pink-cheeked secretary.

"Hope you'll come and see our show some evening. You won't know me at first, because I wear a blond wig in the first scene. Third from the left, front row." And to Mrs. McChesney: "I cer'nly did hate to get up so early this morning, but after you're up it ain't so fierce. And it cer'nly was easy money. Thanks."

Emma McChesney glanced quickly at T. A.,

saw that he was pliant enough for the molding process, and deftly began to shape, and bend, and smooth and pat.

"Let's sit down, and unravel the kinks in our nerves. Now, if you do favor this new plan — oh, I mean after you've given it consideration, and all that! Yes, indeed. But if you do, I think it would be good policy to start the game in — say — Cleveland. The Kaufman-Oster Company of Cleveland have a big, snappy, up-to-the-minute store. We'll get them to send out announcement cards. Something neat and flattering-looking. See? Little stage all framed up. Scene set to show a bedroom or boudoir. Then, thin girls, plump girls, short girls, high girls. They'll go through all the paces. We won't only show the knickerbockers: we demonstrate how the ordinary petticoat bunches and crawls up under the heavy plush and velvet top skirt. We'll show 'em in street clothes, evening clothes, afternoon frocks. Each one in a different shade of satin knicker. And silk stockings and cunning little slippers to match. The store will stand for that. It's a big ad for them, too."

Emma McChesney's hair was slightly tousled.

Her cheeks were carmine. Her eyes glowed.

"Don't you see! Don't you get it! Can't you feel how the thing's going to take hold?"

"By Gad!" burst from T. A. Buck, "I'm darned if I don't believe you're right — almost — But are you sure that you believe —"

Emma McChesney brought one little white fist down into the palm of the other hand. "Sure? Why, I'm so sure that when I shut my eyes I can see T. A. Senior sitting over there in that chair, tapping the side of his nose with the edge of his tortoise-shell-rimmed glasses, and nodding his head, with his features all screwed up like a blessed old gargoyle, the way he always did when something tickled him. That's how sure I am."

T. A. Buck stood up abruptly. He shrugged his shoulders. His face looked strangely white and drawn. "I'll leave it to you. I'll do my share of the work. But I'm not more than half convinced, remember."

"That's enough for the present," answered Emma McChesney, briskly. "Well, now, suppose we talk machinery and girls, and cutters for a while."

Two months later found T. A. Buck and his

sales-manager, both shirt-sleeved, both smoking nervously, as they marked, ticketed, folded, arranged. They were getting out the travelers' spring lines. Entered Mrs. McChesney, and stood eying them, worriedly. It was her dozenth visit to the stock-room that morning. A strange restlessness seemed to trouble her. She wandered from office to show-room, from show-room to factory.

"What's the trouble?" inquired T. A. Buck, squinting up at her through a cloud of cigar smoke.

"Oh, nothing," answered Mrs. McChesney, and stood fingering the piles of glistening satin garments, a queer, faraway look in her eyes. Then she turned and walked listlessly toward the door. There she encountered Spalding — Billy Spalding, of the coveted Middle-Western territory, Billy Spalding, the long-headed, quick-thinking; Spalding, the persuasive, Spalding the mixer, Spalding on whom depended the fate of the T. A. Buck Featherloom Knickerbocker and Pajama.

"'Morning! When do you start out?" she asked him.

"In the morning. Gad, that's some line,

what? I'm itching to spread it. You're certainly a wonder-child, Mrs. McChesney. Why, the boys —"

Emma McChesney sighed, somberly. " That line does sort of — well, tug at your heart-strings, doesn't it? " She smiled, almost wistfully. " Say, Billy, when you reach the Eagle House at Waterloo, tell Annie, the head-waitress to rustle you a couple of Mrs. Traudt's dill pickles. Tell her Mrs. McChesney asked you to. Mrs. Traudt, the proprietor's wife, doles 'em out to her favorites. They're crisp, you know, and firm, and juicy, and cold, and briny."

Spalding drew a sibilant breath. " I'll be there! " he grinned. " I'll be there! "

But he wasn't. At eight the next morning there burst upon Mrs. McChesney a distraught T. A. Buck.

" Hear about Spalding? " he demanded.

" Spalding? No."

" His wife 'phoned from St. Luke's. Taken with an appendicitis attack at midnight. They operated at five this morning. One of those had - it - been - twenty - four - hours - later - etc. operations. That settles us."

"Poor kid," replied Emma McChesney. "Rough on him and his brand-new wife."

"Poor kid! Yes. But how about his territory? How about our new line? How about —"

"Oh, that's all right," said Emma McChesney, cheerfully.

"I'd like to know how! We haven't a man equal to the territory. He's our one best bet."

"Oh, that's all right," said Mrs. McChesney again, smoothly.

A little impatient exclamation broke from T. A. Buck. At that Emma McChesney smiled. Her new listlessness and abstraction seemed to drop from her. She braced her shoulders, and smiled her old sunny, heartening smile.

"I'm going out with that line. I'm going to leave a trail of pajamas and knickerbockers from Duluth to Canton."

"You! No, you won't!" A dull, painful red had swept into T. A. Buck's face. It was answered by a flood of scarlet in Mrs. McChesney's countenance.

"I don't get you," she said. "I'm afraid you don't realize what this trip means. It's going to be a fight. They'll have to be coaxed and bullied and cajoled, and reasoned with. It's going to be a ' show-me ' trip."

T. A. Buck took a quick step forward. " That's just why. I won't have you fighting with buyers, taking their insults, kowtowing to them, salving them. It — it isn't woman's work."

Emma McChesney was sorting the contents of her desk with quick, nervous fingers. " I'll get the Twentieth Century," she said, over her shoulder. " Don't argue, please. If it's no work for a woman then I suppose it follows that I'm unwomanly. For ten years I traveled this country selling T. A. Buck's Featherloom Petticoats. My first trip on the road I was in the twenties — and pretty, too. I'm a woman of thirty-seven now. I'll never forget that first trip — the heartbreaks, the insults I endured, the disappointments, the humiliation, until they understood that I meant business — strictly business. I'm tired of hearing you men say that this and that and the other isn't woman's work. Any work is woman's work that a woman can do well. I've given the ten best years of my life to this firm. Next to my boy at school it's the biggest thing in my life.

" 'Emma McChesney . . . I believe in you now! Dad and I
both believe in you' "—*Page 262*

Sometimes it swamps even him. Don't come to me with that sort of talk." She was locking drawers, searching pigeon-holes, skimming files. " This is my busy day." She arose, and shut her desk with a bang, locked it, and turned a flushed and beaming face toward T. A. Buck, as he stood frowning before her.

" Your father believed in me — from the ground up. We understood each other, he and I. You've learned a lot in the last year and a half, T. A. Junior-that-was, but there's one thing you haven't mastered. When will you learn to believe in Emma McChesney? "

She was out of the office before he had time to answer, leaving him standing there.

In the dusk of a late winter evening just three weeks later, a man paused at the door of the unlighted office marked " Mrs. McChesney." He looked about a moment, as though dreading detection. Then he opened the door, stepped into the dim quiet of the little room, and closed the door gently after him. Everything in the tiny room was quiet, neat, orderly. It seemed to possess something of the character of its absent owner. The intruder stood there a moment, uncertainly, looking about him.

Then he took a step forward and laid one hand on the back of the empty chair before the closed desk. He shut his eyes and it seemed that he felt her firm, cool, reassuring grip on his fingers as they clutched the wooden chair. The impression was so strong that he kept his eyes shut, and they were still closed when his voice broke the silence of the dim, quiet little room.

"Emma McChesney," he was saying aloud, "Emma McChesney, you great big, fine, brave, wonderful woman, you! I believe in you now! Dad and I both believe in you."

X

IN THE ABSENCE OF THE AGENT

THIS is a love-story. But it is a love-story with a logical ending. Which means that in the last paragraph no one has any one else in his arms. Since logic and love have long been at loggerheads, the story may end badly. Still, what love passages there are shall be left intact. There shall be no trickery. There shall be no running breathless, flushed, eager-eyed, to the very gateway of Love's garden, only to bump one's nose against that baffling, impregnable, stone-wall phrase of "let us draw a veil, dear reader." This is the story of the love of a man for a woman, a mother for her son, and a boy for a girl. And there shall be no veil.

Since 8 A. M., when she had unlocked her office door, Mrs. Emma McChesney had been working in bunches of six. Thus, from twelve to one she had dictated six letters, looked up

[263]

memoranda, passed on samples of petticoat silk, fired the office-boy, wired Spalding out in Nebraska, and eaten her lunch. Emma McChesney was engaged in that nerve-racking process known as getting things out of the way. When Emma McChesney aimed to get things out of the way she did not use a shovel; she used a road-drag.

Now, at three-thirty, she shut the last desk-drawer with a bang, locked it, pushed back the desk-phone, discovered under it the inevitable mislaid memorandum, scanned it hastily, tossed the scrap of paper into the brimming waste-basket, and, yawning, raised her arms high above her head. The yawn ended, her arms relaxed, came down heavily, and landed her hands in her lap with a thud. It had been a whirlwind day. At that moment most of the lines in Emma McChesney's face slanted downward.

But only for that moment. The next found her smiling. Up went the corners of her mouth! Out popped her dimples! The laugh-lines appeared at the corners of her eyes. She was still dimpling like an anticipatory child when she had got her wraps from the tiny

"It had been a whirlwind day"—*Page 264*

closet, and was standing before the mirror, adjusting her hat.

The hat was one of those tiny, pert, head-hugging trifles that only a very pretty woman can wear. A merciless little hat, that gives no quarter to a blotched skin, a too large nose, colorless eyes. Emma McChesney stood before the mirror, the cruel little hat perched atop her hair, ready to give it the final and critical bash which should bring it down about her ears where it belonged. But even now, perched grotesquely atop her head as it was, you could see that she was going to get away with it.

It was at this critical moment that the office door opened, and there entered T. A. Buck, president of the T. A. Buck Featherloom Petticoat and Lingerie Company. He entered smiling, leisurely, serene-eyed, as one who anticipates something pleasurable. At sight of Emma McChesney standing, hatted before the mirror, the pleasurable look became less confident.

" Hello! " said T. A. Buck. " Whither? " and laid a sheaf of businesslike-looking papers on the top of Mrs. McChesney's well cleared desk.

IN THE ABSENCE OF THE AGENT

Mrs. McChesney, without turning, performed the cramming process successfully, so that her hat left only a sub-halo of fluffy bright hair peeping out from the brim.

Then, " Playing hooky," she said. " Go 'way."

T. A. Buck picked up the sheaf of papers and stowed them into an inside coat-pocket. " As president of this large and growing concern," he said, " I want to announce that I'm going along."

Emma McChesney adjusted her furs. " As secretary of said firm I rise to state that you're not invited."

T. A. Buck, hands in pockets, stood surveying the bright-eyed woman before him. The pleasurable expression had returned to his face.

" If the secretary of the above-mentioned company has the cheek to play hooky at 3:30 P.M. in the middle of November, I fancy the president can demand to know where she's going, and then go too."

Mrs. McChesney unconcernedly fastened the clasp of her smart English glove.

" Didn't you take two hours for lunch? Had mine off the top of my desk. Ham sandwich and a glass of milk. Dictated six letters between bites and swallows."

A frown of annoyance appeared between T. A. Buck's remarkably fine eyes. He came over to Mrs. McChesney and looked down at her.

"Look here, you'll kill yourself. It's all very well to be interested in one's business, but I draw the line at ruining my digestion for it. Why in Sam Hill don't you take a decent hour at least?"

"Only bricklayers can take an hour for lunch," retorted Emma McChesney. "When you get to be a lady captain of finance you can't afford it."

She crossed to her desk and placed her fingers on the electric switch. The desk-light cast a warm golden glow on the smart little figure in the trim tailored suit, the pert hat, the shining furs. She was rosy-cheeked and bright-eyed as a schoolgirl. There was about her that vigor, and glow, and alert assurance which bespeaks congenial work, sound sleep, healthy digestion, and a sane mind. She was as tingling, and bracing, and alive, and antiseptic as the crisp, snappy November air outdoors.

IN THE ABSENCE OF THE AGENT

T. A. Buck drew a long breath as he looked at her.

"Those are devastating clothes," he remarked. "D'you know, until now I always had an idea that furs weren't becoming to women. Make most of 'em look stuffy. But you —"

Emma McChesney glanced down at the shining skins of muff and scarf. She stroked them gently and lovingly with her gloved hand.

"M-m-m-m! These semi-precious furs *are* rather satisfactory — until you see a woman in sealskin and sables. Then you want to use 'em for a hall rug."

T. A. Buck stepped within the radius of the yellow light, so that its glow lighted up his already luminous eyes — eyes that had a trick of translucence under excitement.

"Sables and sealskin," repeated T. A. Buck, his voice vibrant. "If it's those you want, you can —"

Snap! went the electric switch under Emma McChesney's fingers. It was as decisive as a blow in the face. She walked to the door. The little room was dim.

"I'm sending my boy through college with

[270]

my sealskin-and-sable fund," she said crisply; "and I'm to meet him at 4:30."

"Oh, that's your appointment!" Relief was evident in T. A. Buck's tone.

Emma McChesney shook a despairing head. "For impudent and unquenchable inquisitiveness commend me to a man! Here! If you must know, though I intended it as a surprise when it was finished and furnished — I'm going to rent a flat, a regular six-room, plenty-of-closets flat, after ten years of miserable hotel existence. Jock's running over for two days to approve it. I ought to have waited until the holidays, so he wouldn't miss classes; but I couldn't bear to. I've spent ten Thanksgivings, and ten Christmases, and ten New Years in hotels. Hell has no terrors for me."

They were walking down the corridor together.

"Take me along — please!" pleaded T. A. Buck, like a boy. "I know all about flats, and gas-stoves, and meters, and plumbing, and everything!"

"You!" scoffed Emma McChesney, "with your five-story house and your summer home in the mountains!"

" Mother won't hear of giving up the house. I hate it myself. Bathrooms in those darned old barracks are so cold that a hot tub is an icy plunge before you get to it." They had reached the elevator. A stubborn look appeared about T. A. Buck's jaw. " I'm going!" he announced, and scudded down the hall to his office door. Emma McChesney pressed the elevator-button. Before the ascending car showed a glow of light in the shaft T. A. Buck appeared with hat, gloves, stick.

" I think the car's downstairs. We'll run up in it. What's the address? Seventies, I suppose?"

Emma McChesney stepped out of the elevator and turned. " Car! Not I! If you're bound to come with me you'll take the subway. They're asking enough for that apartment as it is. I don't intend to drive up in a five-thousand-dollar motor and have the agent tack on an extra twenty dollars a month."

T. A. Buck smiled with engaging agreeableness. " Subway it is," he said. " Your presence would turn even a Bronx train into a rose-garden."

Twelve minutes later the new apartment

building, with its cream-tile and red-brick Louis Somethingth façade, and its tan brick and plaster Michael-Dougherty-contractor back, loomed before them, soaring even above its lofty neighbors. On the door-step stood a maple-colored giant in a splendor of scarlet, and gold braid, and glittering buttons. The great entrance door was opened for them by a half-portion duplicate of the giant outside. In the foyer was splendor to grace a palace hall. There were great carved chairs. There was a massive oaken table. There were rugs, there were hangings, there were dim-shaded lamps casting a soft glow upon tapestry and velours.

Awaiting the pleasure of the agent, T. A. Buck, leaning upon his stick, looked about him appreciatively. " Makes the Knickerbocker lobby look like the waiting-room in an orphan asylum."

" Don't let 'em fool you," answered Emma McChesney, *sotto voce*, just before the agent popped out of his office. " It's all included in the rent. Dinky enough up-stairs. If ever I have guests that I want to impress I'll entertain 'em in the hall."

There approached them the agent, smiling,

[273]

urbane, pleasing as to manner — but not too pleasing; urbanity mixed, so to speak, with the leaven of caution.

" Ah, yes! Mrs.— er — McChesney, wasn't it? I can't tell you how many parties have been teasing me for that apartment since you looked at it. I've had to — well — make myself positively unpleasant in order to hold it for you. You said you wished your son to —"

The glittering little jewel-box of an elevator was taking them higher and higher. The agent stared hard at T. A. Buck.

Mrs. McChesney followed his gaze. " My business associate, Mr. T. A. Buck," she said grimly.

The agent discarded caution; he was all urbanity. Their floor attained, he unlocked the apartment door and threw it open with a gesture which was a miraculous mixture of royalty and generosity.

" He knows you! " hissed Emma McChesney, entering with T. A. " Another ten on the rent." The agent pulled up a shade, switched on a light, straightened an electric globe. T. A. Buck looked about at the bare white walls, at the bare polished floor, at the severe fireplace.

[274]

IN THE ABSENCE OF THE AGENT

" I knew it couldn't last," he said.

" If it did," replied Emma McChesney good-naturedly, " I couldn't afford to live here," and disappeared into the kitchen followed by the agent, who babbled ever and anon of views, of Hudsons, of express-trains, of parks, as is the way of agents from Fiftieth Street to One Hundred and 'Umpty-ninth.

T. A. Buck, feet spread wide, hands behind him, was left standing in the center of the empty living-room. He was leaning on his stick and gazing fixedly upward at the ornate chandelier. It was a handsome fixture, and boasted some of the most advanced ideas in modern lighting equipment. Yet it scarcely seemed to warrant the passionate scrutiny which T. A. Buck was bestowing upon it. So rapt was his gaze that when the telephone-bell shrilled unexpectedly in the hallway he started so that his stick slipped on the polished floor, and as Emma McChesney and the still voluble agent emerged from the kitchen the dignified head of the firm of T. A. Buck and Company presented an animated picture, one leg in the air, arms waving wildly, expression at once amazed and hurt.

Emma McChesney surveyed him wide-eyed.

[275]

The agent, unruffled, continued to talk on his way to the telephone.

" It only looks small to you," he was saying. " Fact is, most people think it's too large. They object to a big kitchen. Too much work." He gave his attention to the telephone.

Emma McChesney looked troubled. She stood in the doorway, head on one side, as one who conjures up a mental picture.

" Come here," she commanded suddenly, addressing the startled T. A. " You nagged until I had to take you along. Here's a chance to justify your coming. I want your opinion on the kitchen."

" Kitchens," announced T. A. Buck of the English clothes and the gardenia, " are my specialty," and entered the domain of the gas-range and the sink.

Emma McChesney swept the infinitesimal room with a large gesture.

" Considering it as a kitchen, not as a locker, does it strike you as being adequate? "

T. A. Buck, standing in the center of the room, touched all four walls with his stick.

" I've heard," he ventured, " that they're — ah — using 'em small this year."

Emma McChesney's eyes took on a certain wistful expression. " Maybe. But whenever I've dreamed of a home, which was whenever I got lonesome on the road, which was every evening for ten years, I'd start to plan a kitchen. A kitchen where you could put up preserves, and a keg of dill pickles, and get a full-sized dinner without getting things more than just comfortably cluttered."

T. A. Buck reflected. He flapped his arms as one who feels pressed for room. " With two people occupying the room, as at present, the presence of one dill pickle would sort of crowd things, not to speak of a keg of 'em, and the full-sized dinner, and the — er — preserves. Still —"

" As for a turkey," wailed Emma McChesney, " one would have to go out on the fire-escape to baste it."

The swinging door opened to admit the agent. " Would you excuse me? A party down-stairs — lease — be back in no time. Just look about — any questions — glad to answer later —"

" Quite all right," Mrs. McChesney assured him. Her expression was one of relief as the hall door closed behind him. " Good! There's a spot in the mirror over the mantel. I've been dying to find out if it was a flaw in the glass or only a smudge."

She made for the living-room. T. A. Buck followed thoughtfully. Thoughtfully and interestedly he watched her as she stood on tiptoe, breathed stormily upon the mirror's surface, and rubbed the moist place with her handkerchief. She stood back a pace, eyes narrowed critically.

" It's gone, isn't it ? " she asked.

T. A. Buck advanced to where she stood and cocked his head too, judicially, and in the opposite direction to which Emma McChesney's head was cocked. So that the two heads were very close together.

" It's a poor piece of glass," he announced at last.

A simple enough remark. Perhaps it was made with an object in view, but certainly it was not meant to bring forth the storm of protest that came from Emma McChesney's lips. She turned on him, lips quivering, eyes wrathful.

" You shouldn't have come ! " she cried. " You're as much out of place in a six-room flat as a truffle would be in a boiled New England dinner. Do you think I don't see its short-comings? Every normal woman, no matter what sort of bungalow, palace, ranch-house, cave, cottage, or tenement she may be living in, has in her mind's eye a picture of the sort of apartment she'd live in if she could afford it. I've had mine mapped out from the wall-paper in the front hall to the laundry-tubs in the base-ment, and it doesn't even bear a family resem-blance to this."

"I'm sorry," stammered T. A. Buck. "You asked my opinion and I —"

"Opinion! If every one had so little tact as to give their true opinion when it was asked this would be a miserable world. I asked you be-cause I wanted you to lie. I expected it of you. I needed bolstering up. I realize that the rent I'm paying and the flat I'm getting form a geo-metrical problem where X equals the unknown quantity and only the agent knows the answer. But it's going to be a home for Jock and me. It's going to be a place where he can bring his friends; where he can have his books, and his 'baccy, and his college junk. It will be the first real home that youngster has known in all his

[279]

miserable boarding-house, hotel, boys' school, and college existence. Sometimes when I think of what he's missed, of the loneliness and the neglect when I was on the road, of the barrenness of his boyhood, I —"

T. A. Buck started forward as one who had made up his mind about something long considered. Then he gulped, retreated, paced excitedly to the door and back again. On the return trip he found smiling and repentant Emma McChesney regarding him.

" Now aren't you sorry you insisted on coming along? Letting yourself in for a ragging like that? I think I'm a wee bit taut in the nerves at the prospect of seeing Jock — and planning things with him — I —"

T. A. Buck paused in his pacing. " Don't! " he said. " I had it coming to me. I did it deliberately. I wanted to know how you really felt about it."

Emma McChesney stared at him curiously. " Well, now you know. But I haven't told you half. In all those years while I was selling T. A. Buck's Featherloom Petticoats on the road, and eating hotel food that tasted the same, whether it was roast beef or ice-cream, I was planning this little place. I've even made up my mind to the scandalous price I'm willing to pay a maid who'll cook real dinners for us and serve them as I've always vowed Jock's dinners should be served when I could afford something more than a shifting hotel home."

T. A. Buck was regarding the head of his walking-stick with a gaze as intent as that which he previously had bestowed upon the chandelier. For that matter it was a handsome enough stick — a choice thing in malacca. But it was scarcely more deserving than the chandelier had been.

Mrs. McChesney had wandered into the dining-room. She peered out of windows. She poked into butler's pantry. She inspected wall-lights. And still T. A. Buck stared at his stick.

" It's really robbery," came Emma McChesney's voice from the next room. " Only a New York agent could have the nerve to do it. I've a friend who lives in Chicago — Mary Cutting. You've heard me speak of her. Has a flat on the north side there, just next door to the lake. The rent is ridiculous; and — would you believe it? — the flat is equipped with bookcases, and gorgeous mantel shelves, and buffet, and bathroom fixtures, and china-closets, and hall-tree —"

Her voice trailed into nothingness as she disappeared into the kitchen. When she emerged again she was still enumerating the charms of the absurdly low-priced Chicago flat, thus:

" — and full-length mirrors, and wonderful folding table-shelf gimcracks in the kitchen, and —"

T. A. Buck did not look up. But, "Oh, Chicago!" he might have been heard to murmur, as only a New-Yorker can breathe those two words.

"Don't 'Oh, Chicago!' like that," mimicked Emma McChesney. "I've lain awake nights dreaming of a home I once saw there, with the lake in the back yard, and a couple of miles of veranda, and a darling vegetable-garden, and the whole place simply honeycombed with bathrooms, and sleeping-porches, and sun-parlors, and linen-closets, and — gracious, I wonder what's keeping Jock!"

T. A. Buck wrenched his eyes from his stick. All previous remarks descriptive of his eyes under excitement paled at the glow which lighted them now. They glowed straight into

Emma McChesney's eyes and held them, startled.

"Emma," said T. A. Buck quite calmly, "will you marry me? I want to give you all those things, beginning with the lake in the back yard and ending with the linen-closets and the sun-parlor."

And Emma McChesney, standing there in the middle of the dining-room floor, stared long at T. A. Buck, standing there in the center of the living-room floor. And if any human face, in the space of seventeen seconds, could be capable of expressing relief, and regret, and alarm, and dismay, and tenderness, and wonder, and a great womanly sympathy, Emma McChesney's countenance might be said to have expressed all those emotions — and more. The last two were uppermost as she slowly came toward him.

"T. A.," she said, and her voice had in it a marvelous quality, "I'm thirty-nine years old. You know I was married when I was eighteen and got my divorce after eight years. Those eight years would have left any woman who had endured them with one of two determinations: to take up life again and bring it out into the sunshine until it was sound, and sweet, and clean, and whole once more, or to hide the hurt and brood over it, and cover it with bitterness, and hate until it destroyed by its very foulness. I had Jock, and I chose the sun, thank God! I said then that marriage was a thing tried and abandoned forever, for me. And now —"

There was something almost fine in the lines of T. A. Buck's too feminine mouth and chin; but not fine enough.

"Now, Emma," he repeated, "will you marry me?"

Emma McChesney's eyes were a wonderful thing to see, so full of pain were they, so wide with unshed tears.

"As long as — he — lived," she went on, "the thought of marriage was repulsive to me. Then, that day seven months ago out in Iowa, when I picked up that paper and saw it staring out at me in print that seemed to waver and dance "— she covered her eyes with her hand for a moment —"' McChesney — Stuart McChesney, March 7, aged forty-seven years. Funeral to-day from Howland Brothers' chapel. Aberdeen and Edinburgh papers please copy!'"

"'Emma,' he said, 'will you marry me?'"—*Page 287*

IN THE ABSENCE OF THE AGENT

T. A. Buck took the hand that covered her eyes and brought it gently down.

"Emma," he said, "will you marry me?"

"T. A., I don't love you. Wait! Don't say it! I'm thirty-nine, but I'm brave and foolish enough to say that all these years of work, and disappointment, and struggle, and bitter experience haven't convinced me that love does not exist. People have said about me, seeing me in business, that I'm not a marrying woman. There is no such thing as that. Every woman is a marrying woman, and sometimes the lightheartedest, and the scoffingest, and the most self-sufficient of us are, beneath it all, the marryingest. Perhaps I'm making a mistake. Perhaps ten years from now I'll be ready to call myself a fool for having let slip what the wise ones would call a 'chance.' But I don't think so, T. A."

"You know me too well," argued T. A. Buck rather miserably. "But at least you know the worst of me as well as the best. You'd be taking no risks."

Emma McChesney walked to the window. There was a little silence. Then she finished it with one clean stroke. "We've been good business chums, you and I. I hope we always shall be. I can imagine nothing more beautiful on this earth for a woman than being married to a man she cares for and who cares for her. But, T. A., you're not the man."

And then there were quick steps in the corridor, a hand at the door-knob, a slim, tall figure in the doorway. Emma McChesney seemed to waft across the rooms and into the embrace of the slim, tall figure.

" Welcome — home ! " she cried. " Sketch in the furniture to suit yourself."

" This is going to be great — great ! " announced Jock. " What do you know about the Oriental potentate down-stairs ! I guess Otis Skinner has nothing on him when it comes — Why, hello, Mr. Buck ! " He was peering into the next room. " Why don't you folks light up ? I thought you were another agent person. Met that one down in the hall. Said he'd be right up. What's the matter with him anyway ? He smiles like a waxworks. When the elevator took me up he was still smiling from the foyer, and I could see his grin after the rest of him was lost to sight. Regular Cheshire. What's this ? Droring-room ? "

JAMES MONTGOMERY FLAGG

" 'Welcome home!' she cried. 'Sketch in the furniture to suit yourself' "—*Page 288*

He rattled on like a pleased boy. He strode over to shake hands with Buck. Emma McChesney, cheeks glowing, eyed him adoringly. Then she gave a little suppressed cry.

" Jock, what's happened? "

Jock whirled around like a cat. " Where? When? What? "

Emma McChesney pointed at him with one shaking finger. " You! You're thin! You're — you're emaciated. Your shoulders, where are they? Your — your legs —"

Jock looked down at himself. His glance was pride. " Clothes," he said.

" Clothes? " faltered his mother.

" You're losing your punch, Mother? You used to be up on men's rigging. All the boys look like their own shadows these days. English cut. No padding. No heels. Incurve at the waist. Watch me walk." He flapped across the room, chest concave, shoulders rounded, arms hanging limp, feet wide apart, chin thrust forward.

" Do you mean to tell me that's your present form of locomotion? " demanded his mother.

" I hope so. Been practising it for weeks. They call it the juvenile jump, and all our best

[289]

leading men have it. I trailed Douglas Fairbanks for days before I really got it."

And the tension between T. A. Buck and Emma McChesney snapped with a jerk, and they both laughed, and laughed again, at Jock's air of offended dignity. They laughed until the rancor in the heart of the man and the hurt and pity in the heart of the woman melted into a bond of lasting understanding.

" Go on — laugh ! " said Jock. " Say, Mother, is there a shower in the bathroom, h'm?" And was off to investigate.

The laughter trailed away into nothingness. " Jock," called his mother, " do you want your bedroom done in plain or stripes?"

" Plain," came from the regions beyond. " Got a lot of pennants and everything."

T. A. Buck picked up his stick from the corner in which it stood.

" I'll run along," he said. " You two will want to talk things over together." He raised his voice to reach the boy in the other room. " I'm off, Jock."

Jock's protest sounded down the hall. " Don't leave me alone with her. She'll blarney me into consenting to blue-and-pink rosebud paper in my bedroom."

T. A. Buck had the courage to smile even at that. Emma McChesney was watching him, her clear eyes troubled, anxious.

At the door Buck turned, came back a step or two. " I — I think, if you don't mind, I'll play hooky this time and run over to Atlantic City for a couple of days. You'll find things slowing up, now that the holidays are so near."

" Fine idea — fine! " agreed Emma McChesney; but her eyes still wore the troubled look.

" Good-by," said T. A. Buck abruptly.

" Good —" and then she stopped. " I've a brand-new idea. Give you something to worry about on your vacation."

" I'm supplied," answered T. A. Buck grimly.

" Nonsense! A real worry. A business worry. A surprise."

Jock had joined them, and was towering over his mother, her hand in his.

T. A. Buck regarded them moodily. " After your pajama and knickerbocker stunt I'm braced for anything."

"Nothing theatrical this time," she assured him. "Don't expect a show such as you got when I touched off the last fuse."

An eager, expectant look was replacing the gloom that had clouded his face. "Spring it."

Emma McChesney waited a moment; then, "I think the time has come to put in another line — a staple. It's — flannel nightgowns."

"Flannel nightgowns!" Disgust shivered through Buck's voice. *"Flannel nightgowns!* They quit wearing those when Broadway was a cow-path."

"Did, eh?" retorted Emma McChesney. "That's the New-Yorker speaking. Just because the French near-actresses at the Winter Garden wear silk lace and sea-foam nighties in their imported boudoir skits, and just because they display only those frilly, beribboned hand-made affairs in the Fifth Avenue shop-windows, don't you ever think that they're a national vice. Let me tell you," she went on as T. A. Buck's demeanor grew more bristlingly antagonistic, "there are thousands and thousands of women up in Minnesota, and Wisconsin, and Michigan, and Oregon, and Alaska, and Nebraska, and Dakota who are thankful to retire every night protected by one long, thick, serviceable flannel nightie, and one practical hot-water bag. Up in those countries retiring isn't a social rite: it's a feat of hardihood. I'm keen for a line of plain, full, roomy old-fashioned flannel nightgowns of the improved T. A. Buck Featherloom products variety. They'll be wearing 'em long after knickerbockers have been cut up for patchwork."

The moody look was quite absent from T. A. Buck's face now, and the troubled look from Emma McChesney's eyes.

"Well," Buck said grudgingly, "if you were to advise making up a line of the latest models in deep-sea divers' uniforms, I suppose I'd give in. But flannel nightgowns! In the twentieth century — flannel night —"

"Think it over," laughed Emma McChesney as he opened the door. "We'll have it out, tooth and nail, when you get back."

The door closed upon him. Emma McChesney and her son were left alone in their new home to be.

"Turn out the light, son," said Emma McChesney, "and come to the window. There's a view! Worth the money, alone."

IN THE ABSENCE OF THE AGENT

Jock switched off the light. " D' you know, Blonde, I shouldn't wonder if old T. A.'s sweetish on you," he said as he came over to the window.

" Old ! "

" He's forty or over, isn't he ? "

" Son, do you realize your charming mother's thirty-nine ? "

" Oh, you ! That's different. You look a kid. You're young in all the spots where other women of thirty-nine look old. Around the eyes, and under the chin, and your hands, and the corners of your mouth."

In the twilight Emma McChesney turned to stare at her son. " Just where did you learn all that, young 'un ? At college ? "

And, " Some view, isn't it, Mother ? " parried Jock. The two stood there, side by side, looking out across the great city that glittered and swam in the soft haze of the late November afternoon. There are lovelier sights than New York seen at night, from a window eyrie with a mauve haze softening all, as a beautiful but experienced woman is softened by an artfully draped scarf of chiffon. There are cities of roses, cities of mountains, cities of palm-trees and sparkling lakes; but no sight, be it of mountains, or roses, or lakes, or waving palm-trees, is more likely to cause that vague something which catches you in the throat.

It caught those two home-hungry people. And it opened the lips of one of them almost against his will.

" Mother," said Jock haltingly, painfully, " I came mighty near coming home — for good — this time."

His mother turned and searched his face in the dim light.

" What was it, Jock? " she asked, quite without fuss.

The slim young figure in the jumping juvenile clothes stirred and tried to speak, tried again, formed the two words: " A — girl."

Emma McChesney waited a second, until the icy, cruel, relentless hand that clutched her very heart should have relaxed ever so little. Then, " Tell me, sonny boy," she said.

" Why, Mother — that girl —" There was an agony of bitterness and of disillusioned youth in his voice.

Emma McChesney came very close, so that her head, in the pert little close-fitting hat, rested on the boy's shoulder. She linked her arm through his, snug and warm.

" That girl —" she echoed encouragingly.

And, " That girl," went on Jock, taking up the thread of his grief, " why, Mother, that — girl —"

THE END

University of Illinois Press
1325 South Oak Street
Champaign, IL 61820-6903
www.press.uillinois.edu